WHAT'S THE POINT OF

by

CHRIS WEST

"Quiet people have the loudest minds."
Stephen Hawking

Copyright © Chris West 2020
Published by CWTK Publications
Cover design by Chris Howard blondesign@gmail.com

All rights reserved by the author. This is a work of fiction. Names, characters, businesses, places, events and incidents are either the products of the author's imagination or used in a fictitious manner. Any resemblance to actual persons, living or dead, is purely coincidental.

Longing

She stands there: a plain, chubby girl with glasses, Brillo-pad hair and a sensible outfit, apart from some platform boots that still pinch her feet though she's had them of over a month, and a real (according to the stallholder on Lewisham market) artist's beret. Before her are the gates of the Polytechnic of the South Circular, and above them is an inscription, at which she is gazing.

KNOWLEDGE FOR ALL.

She feels a lump in her throat. This might be thanks to the *Gauloises* she has recently started smoking, but it's much more than that. It's excitement. And fear. A lot of fear. This (as they say) is the first day of the rest of her life.

I know all this, because it's me. A long time ago. October 1st, 1974. My first day at college.

Lucy – she's my sister – says that the Poly is 'crap', and that she's either going to Oxford University where she'll marry an aristocrat or to Chelsea College of Art where she'll take lots of drugs and become famous. Mother, on the other hand, is amazed that the Poly has accepted me at all: I wasn't exactly a shining light at school, was I?

Nobody is impressed by the course I've chosen, Liberal Arts. Lucy says art should be illiberal, the prerogative of a brilliant elite. Mr Brown, a bank manager whom Mother sees far too often for my liking, says that studying such airy-fairy stuff is self-indulgent, especially given the current economic climate.

Well, pooh to the lot of them. I'll be studying literature, music, art and – how about this? – philosophy.

Philosophy, from the Greek *'philo'* which means 'love of' and *'sophos'* which means 'wisdom'. Plain, chubby, Brillo-haired, not-exactly-a-shining-light-at-school Stella is about to become a philosopher.

I give my beret a touch more tilt and push the strap of my shoulder-bag up a bit – it is thrillingly heavy with books – then march in through the gates.

*

My first lecture!

I sit right at the front as I don't want to miss a single word. I set out my stuff: my beret (or should I say *mon beret?*), my Students' A4 Notepad, my day-glo pink biro (a present from Lucy), my shiny new course textbook, *The Analytical Method, A Brief Introduction to Logical Heuristics* by Dr Caradoc Peabody PhD (Cantab). The book is shiny because I haven't managed to get past page three. But never mind, the author is speaking to us in seven minutes' time – six, now – so all will soon become clear.

The room begins to fill. Nobody else sits right at the front.

See? Already, I'm not fitting in. Nobody in our family has ever been to a place of Higher Education. Mother says people shouldn't get 'ideas above their station', at which point Lucy always makes the same joke about does she mean Sydenham or Penge East. I've always disliked this notion – but maybe she's right.

Phew! An older lady – she must be at least 25 – is making her way down the row. She is wearing denims and a baggy, striped sweater covered in badges. "Hi," she says, taking a seat one away from me. "I'm Anna."

"Oh, er, I'm Stella."

"Exciting, isn't it?"

"Yes!" I exclaim, then don't know what to say next.

"Nice beret," she says after a long pause.

"*Merci*," I reply.

Was that a touch pretentious?

Oui, I suddenly know, but luckily I'm saved from further embarrassment by the sound of footsteps on the podium.

I have been imagining what a philosopher will look like. A beard. A leather jacket. Shades, which he will remove at some point to reveal penetrating, world-weary eyes.

Dr Caradoc Peabody PhD (Cantab) is wearing a tweed jacket, trousers made out of some kind of polyester, a bow tie and wire-rimmed glasses. He's clean-shaven, though looks like he got a couple of nicks this morning.

'Oh, Stella, you can be so superficial!' I tell myself angrily. This man is a philosopher. It his mind, not his choice in fabrics, I have come here to study.

Dr Peabody strides to the lectern – well, he just walks, actually – places his notes on it and looks round the room. "Good morning, students," he says. A globule of spit lands on my Student's A4 Notepad. "What do you think this course is about?" Another globule lands, a couple of inches closer to me than the first one. I think it's the Ts that do it.

"Philosophy," says someone.

"Correct. Can we be a bit more specific? What is philosophy about?"

The globules are getting bigger and closer, but I don't care; I'd drown in spit to become a philosopher.

"Wisdom," says a voice near me. Anna's. I suddenly

want her to be my best friend, and regret lapsing into French all the more.

However, Dr Peabody doesn't seem impressed by Anna's answer. "Wisdom?" he echoes back in a querulous tone.

"Right and wrong?" says another voice.

"Right and wrong?" The same tone. Clearly our answers are too obvious. Too shallow. Too *jejeune*.

"The meaning of life?" says a third student.

Now that's got it, surely. But the philosopher just frowns. My God, this is going to be so deep!

A silence falls, profound and existential. I imagine they have silences like this on the *Rive Gauche*, when Jean-Paul Sartre has raised a particularly baffling question.

"What do all the answers you have given me have in common? Think, everybody, think!" (Ks have the spit-projecting effect too, though fortunately not quite as powerful.)

"They're words," says a male voice from the back.

I repress a giggle. Typical of the stupidest kind of guy – showing off; thinks he's funny when everyone else knows he's an idiot.

A grin creeps across the doctor's face. No doubt he's thought of some brilliant put-down.

"At last!" he says finally. "A philosophical answer. They are words. Which is what philosophy is about. Words. What do we mean when we use words? One of you said 'the meaning of life'. What did you mean by the word 'meaning'?" He stares at the unfortunate individual who made the suggestion.

"Well, er, what it's for," she stammers back.

"What's it's *for*," Dr Peabody echoes, his grin expanding. "What do you mean by 'for'?"

"Er, dunno... What's the point of it all?"

"The *point* of it all?" says Peabody gleefully. He extracts a pencil from his jacket pocket and jabs it into the least fleshless bit of his thumb. "What is the point of this pencil? It has a point, but what is the point of it? If I write with it sufficiently so that it becomes blunt, does it still have a point? Has it become a pointless pencil?"

Nobody replies.

"This troublesome ambiguity occurs because 'point' is a word. This is a point. You could say I am pointing at the point. But the word 'point' is not a point. Which is exactly my point."

He pauses, lost in his own delight, then comes back to earth.

"In this series of lectures, I want to look at some of the ways we use – and abuse – words, and what philosophers have done to bring clarity – and, sadly, obscurity – to the proceedings. As I said in my book..."

*

"Bollocks!" says Anna as we sit down in the refectory with two Styrofoam cups of coffee.

"He's supposed to be the expert."

"Expert, my arse." Anna looks me full in the eye, daring me to contradict her. I feel a wave of reassurance.

But waves splatter onto beaches and turn to froth. *Sydenham or Penge East, Stella?*

"I don't think Dr Peabrain has the answers *we* are looking for," Anna continues.

"No," I reply, cresting a mighty new wave.

Anna takes a sip of coffee. "God, this stuff's revolting. Now, what's next? Ah. *Literature 101*. Should be more like it! Philosophy, the way they do it here, anyway, is just a lot of middle-aged men quibbling about words. Literature is about life. Love, ambition, loyalty, betrayal!"

I want to learn more about these things.

*

We get to the lecture theatre early, but don't sit right at the front in case Dr D Spigott has the same spittle-control problem as Dr Peabody. The room fills. Time passes. Students begin whispering to one another. Anna starts packing her pens away and mutters about trying the Union bar – then a side door opens and a man in scruffy jeans and a donkey jacket walks in. He looks like he's come to fix something, but heads for the lectern.

"Hello," he begins, once he's there. "How many of you actually enjoy literature? Old novels, poetry, that sort of thing."

Anna puts her hand up at once. I follow her.

"I hate it," Dr D Spigott continues. "We are in the middle of the Ultimate Crisis of Late Capitalism, and what do I find on this reading list? Jane Austen: petty bourgeois tittle-tattle. DH Lawrence: fascist sympathizer and traitor to the working class. TS Eliot: the pseudo-mystical outpourings of an anti-Semitic bank clerk... Luckily for you, I have something more substantial." He produces a small red book and waves it at us. "The Thoughts of Chairman Mao Tse Tung!"

*

After lunch, we have *Introduction to Music* from a Dr S Licht. I say I'm not going, but Anna says I must give it a chance. So I do.

The lecturer appears on time, which puts him ahead of Dr Spigott, but he looks terribly old. As he shuffles across the stage, I begin to wonder if he'll make it to the lectern before he has an unpleasant accident and has to be wheeled off to Lewisham General.

Sydenham or Penge East, Stella?

He finally reaches his goal – hurrah! – and begins to speak. "Good afternoon, everybody." Actually, his voice is pretty robust. "I'm here to teach you the History of Music. In a series of ten lectures of an hour each. This is, of course, a completely impossible task."

Oh, God. Here we go again.

"The study of music is, at its deepest, an investigation into what it means to be human," he continues. "It is about what it means to live, what it means to feel joy, wonder, love and pain. It is also a study of history, of how events and cultures have moulded the human psyche in different ways. It is a study of theology, of our relationship to the divine. It is a study of psychology: what manner of creature are we, that we can create and love great music? It is, perhaps most of all, a study of philosophy, of the great moral and directional questions of human life… So ten one-hour lectures are hardly going to be enough. But I shall do my best."

I turn to Anna, who turns to me at exactly the same time with exactly the same look of triumph.

*

Next day, I'm walking from the library to the refectory, when I see Dr Licht ahead of me. I am overcome by my usual shyness, but I make myself run and catch him up.

"My friend and I really liked your lecture," I say.

"Oh. Thank you."

"It's full of – gosh, I don't know how to say this – interesting thoughts about the meaning of life and art and philosophy and all that sort of thing."

"You're most kind."

I feel emboldened. "I don't really understand our actual philosophy course."

He nods. "But you are interested in the subject?"

"Yes. Very much."

"I'm glad," he says, then falls silent. And actually, that is the end of the conversation, apart from a polite 'goodbye', as after the next swing doors (the Poly is full of swing doors) we have to go in different directions.

*

Joe is sitting in his corner with his usual extra-strong tea. *Ballroom Blitz* by Sweet is playing on the radio.

"So how's it going?" asks Carlo.

"OK," I reply hesitantly.

The café is my second home. I waitressed here for a year before starting my academic adventure.

Carlo frowns. "OK? Is that all?"

"Yes…" I reply.

Dr Licht's lecture was amazing, but as I watched him shuffle away after those swing doors, I felt that was my future shuffling away: uncomprehended, maybe incomprehensible. *Stella is a bit of a dreamer*, my reports used to say. *Stella lacks the aptitude for proper study.* Now I just hope the old boy forgets the conversation ever occurred.

"Life should be more than 'OK', Stella," says Carlo. "It should be amazing. You'll always be welcome back here if being a student just stays 'OK'. We had fun!"

"That's... very nice," I reply.

We did, too, but I always felt I wanted more. It seems that was a delusion. Green grass on the other side of a fence, which turned out to be plastic.

Ballroom Blitz fades out and is replaced by a live studio debate on platform heels. Have they become too high? No, says Trisha from Greenford.

I light a *Gauloise* and start coughing.

*

Dr Licht's next lecture is about mediaeval music – and mediaeval theology, history, painting and literature, the life of Hildegard of Bingen and an analogy between the Holy Roman Empire and the debate about whether Britain should remain in the Common Market, which it joined last year. I look up at the clock, and see with heartbreak that it is time to finish.

"Before I go – I have been asked by one of you – I can't see you – Oh, yes, there you are – to say more about philosophy and its relationship to music. Sadly, there is not time for me to do this properly, and you already have an excellent Introduction to Philosophy course. However, I do not wish to disappoint the young lady, or anyone else with a similar curiosity: I would be happy to give some informal seminars on the subject for the rest of this term. If anyone is interested, I shall be in my office at 6.30 tomorrow evening."

Belonging

I turn up early just in case there's a crowd, but actually I'm the first and it only ends up with six of us. Me, Anna, a couple of other girls about whom I now remember nothing (sorry, ladies, if you're reading this now), and two males: a rather sad-looking older man – like Anna, way into his twenties – whom Anna immediately nicknames Big Ears for obvious reasons, and a mousy lad in a purple shirt and flared trousers, who inevitably ends up as Noddy.

Maybe it's just as well we are so few, as Dr Licht's office isn't very big. It's also very full: with a piano, a violin, music stands, scores, loose sheets of music paper, a bust of WA Mozart, boxes of tape, an old reel-to-reel tape recorder with Bakelite buttons, a pair of loudspeakers with torn fronts, and, most of all, with books. There are books on music, books on philosophy, books on history, books on psychology, books on religion, books on sociology, books on art, books full of poetry, books I haven't a clue what they're about. There's a complete Shakespeare, six volumes of Gibbon's *Decline and Fall of the Roman Empire*, half a shelf of European novels I've heard of but know shamefully little about: *Madame Bovary, Anna Karenina, Crime and Punishment*. The books are piled in corners. Dr Licht's desk-lamp sits on four books (about mediaeval history). There are books under the tape-recorder, books under Anna's seat, books behind the door. The place even smells of books, which might seem musty and boring to some people but which to me is intoxicating.

The Doctor glances at his watch and asks Anna to

close the door.

"Welcome to what I'm going to call my Enlightenment Club," he begins once she is back in her seat. "I'm afraid I was dishonest when I spoke to the class as a whole. I do *not* consider the lectures given by the Philosophy Department 'excellent' at all. I consider them to have betrayed both the great thinkers of the past and – even more seriously – the curious young minds of the future."

He looks round at us proudly. "Philosophy is a quest, not a word game. It's a quest that began when one of our distant ancestors looked around and began to wonder. What? When? How? Why? The last, above all: why? The quest shall end… Well, we shall see that it has no end, and will never have one as long as there are human beings on this earth."

My beret is in my bag, and I give it a little squeeze.

"In these sessions we can only eavesdrop on a tiny part of the great human quest," Dr Licht goes on. "Apologies to any Hellenophiles, Senecans, mediaevalists or anyone interested in the world's many other great intellectual traditions: Hinduism, Islam, Buddhism, Confucianism. Time compels me to start in Europe, at the dawning of what we call the modern age. In 1619, a young Frenchman is sitting by a stove on a winter day, lost in puzzlement. He wants to know what to dedicate himself to. Science? Religion? Are these compatible? And, more deeply, how could he know if they were? What does it mean when he says he 'knows' something? He is not just picking over the minutiae of language; he wants to engage with life with the full force of his intelligence. In other words, he is a true philosopher."

'Like us,' I think. The six of us, who have made the effort to step out of the run of things and come here to learn…

"The generation of thinkers before our *penseur* had been particularly troubled by the last of the young man's questions: how do you know when you know something? For them, true knowledge was impossible; in the end, you either relied on faith or you faced the philosopher's nightmare – nihilism. Nihilism means that nothing that we or anyone else can assert or believe has any absolute, guaranteed validity or meaning. Anyone who has *truly* experienced this state of mind will tell you it is terrifying."

The Doctor pauses to let this sink in, then recommences. "Our young man – his name is René Descartes by the way – does *not* want to end up with nihilism. But he won't accept easy answers. He will doubt everything he can, and see if there is anything left. Anything at all. If there isn't, he will accept nihilism with all its anguish."

Dr Licht takes us on Descartes' journey of doubt. Can we trust our senses? No, we misidentify things all the time. So what about abstract, logical structures? In mathematics, things can be proven – but what is proof? Maybe there's a demon, trying to fool us into believing something to be 'proven' that is actually false. Can we even prove we exist? Maybe this demon is fooling us about this, too.

I give myself a reassuring pinch. I exist.

But supposing a demon is making me think I've just felt a pinch?

Oh. Scary. Perhaps I'm not cut out for this philosophy stuff after all…

"Of course, Descartes did find an answer," the Doctor continues, "or we wouldn't be talking about him now. Does anyone know what it was?"

"*Cogito ergo sum,*" pipes up a familiar voice.

"Thank you, Anna. *Cogito ergo sum.* I think, therefore I am. You can doubt the truth of any thought, but you can't deny there's thinking going on. So something must be doing the thinking. So I, as the thinker, must exist. Clever, eh?"

Of course I can be a philosopher! Demons – what a ridiculous idea!

"Having established a point of certainty," Dr Licht goes on, "Descartes went on to build a system on it, one that both explained the world – or at least provided the tools to explain it – and generated a moral code by which to run his life. How well he did this, we shall consider next week, but for now I want you just to ponder his basic method. *Find one point of absolute certainty, then build on it.* That, ladies and gentlemen, is the basic technique of philosophy. It has nothing to do with playing around with words."

He lets us digest that thought for a moment, then reaches across to the tape recorder.

"You may be wondering if it has anything to do with music. An excellent question and a true philosopher's one. It is one that I shall answer… another time. Right now, let's just listen to some music."

He pushes a button. The reels creak; the speakers hiss.

"Ladies and gentlemen," says the Doctor, "I present to you the *Requiem* of Wolfgang Amadeus Mozart."

*

"Hi Stella," says Carlo. "You look happy."

"I am."

"Great!" He pauses. "Don't tell me! You've fallen in love!"

"In a way." I remove *le beret* and place it proudly in front of me. Carlo looks puzzled, then asks if I want my usual milky coffee.

"Yes, please. That's one thing the Poly can't do!"

He disappears behind the espresso machine. "So, tell me," he says over the hisses and gurgles.

"It's this group. We talk about such interesting things. We listen to wonderful music. Mozart's *Requiem*. Ever heard it?"

"That sort of stuff never did much for me."

Tiger Feet by Mud comes on the radio.

"You should. It's… amazing," I tell him. "The Doctor turned on this old tape recorder, and this music came out of it. It was sad, but sort of happy in its own way too. Then voices joined in, so lovely and pure. They swirled around, and grew and grew till they came to this incredible climax. It turned me inside out; it was so beautiful."

"Sounds good," says Carlo.

"I'm a philosopher, too."

"Ah. What is your philosophy?"

"I haven't got one yet. Philosophy is more a way of looking at things. A method. Find one point of absolute certainty – a Cartesian point, we call it, after René Descartes – and build on it."

"Ah." Carlo brings the coffee. It feels odd being waited on by my former boss, but he seems happy enough. Not that anything ever seems to get him down, not even that trouble with the food inspectors last Christmas.

"Descartes went on this journey of doubt," I continue. "He refused to accept anything that could be doubted. Anything – sense impressions, mathematics, logic – even the fact that he existed."

"Sounds a bit of a nutter to me."

"No, well, he came up with this formula, something he couldn't doubt. *Cogito ergo sum*. I think, therefore I am."

He looks puzzled. "You are what?"

"Just 'I am'. I think therefore I am."

"Oh."

Silence falls, apart from Mud, another gurgle from the machine and two cars hooting at each other on the South Circular Road outside.

"It suits you, Stella."

"What?"

"Mozart's whatsit. All that thinking therefore you are, even if you don't seem to be anything in particular. All that brainy stuff."

"They said I was stupid at school."

"I never thought that, Stella. Schools are stupid."

*

By the end of the Club's next session, Descartes' attempt to build systematic thought on his *cogito* are in tatters.

OK, thinking is going on, but what else can you deduce from that? *I* think, but what is this 'I'? A discrete individual or a deluded part of something bigger?

Never mind, the Doctor insists, it's the method that matters.

Instead, we look at the work of Descartes' great rival, the British 'empiricist', John Locke. He had a point of certainty, too, and a much simpler one than Descartes' maxim. Truth comes to us though our senses.

"Simple!" says the Doctor, tapping the tape recorder with a biro. "That noise was real; the pen is real, the tape recorder is real. OK, our senses can mislead us sometimes, but over time the errors cancel out. We can use what we sense to build a picture of reality that we can really trust."

I spend the next week wondering what all the philosophical fuss is about – but at the next session the Doctor introduces a Scotsman, David Hume, who points out that our senses tell us nothing beyond the moment.

The Doctor does the tap again. "All we actually *know* – at the moment of experience only – is that some event is happening in our brain." Another tap. "Tapping noise, then. Everything else…" He gives a big shrug. "Do things cause other things? Maybe. Or maybe the world is just one big jumble of coincidences. We don't know. And as for right versus wrong, or ugliness versus beauty – these are just emotional reactions, with no objective value or meaning. If you like the sound of chalk on a blackboard and I like Mozart's *Requiem*, that's just how we are, and there is nothing more to be said."

"Isn't this nihilism?" Anna asks.

"Yes. But Hume didn't seem to mind. His advice was to go for a nice long walk, forget about it and get on with day-to-day life. Of course, I can't accept that answer."

"So what do we do?"

"Wait till next week. Let's listen to some more music."

*

The week races by. Then we meet Karl Marx. He suggested that ultimate truth was found in history, more specifically in the struggle between the classes. Class power spreads itself into all areas of life, not just how we work and earn, but how we think, know and feel.

At Dr Spigott's next lecture, I sit in the front row and mutter 'right on' at regular intervals – but at the next Club meeting, Dr Licht says that history actually shows Marx to be fatally flawed. He made loads of predictions, virtually none of which have come true. But if you point that out to Marxists, they will tell you that you are suffering from 'false consciousness'. Marx's system has its own inbuilt logic that makes it impossible to criticize. You are either a True Believer or an outsider.

"This puts Marxism on a par with the delusions of cult leaders," the Doctor continues. "So we have to look elsewhere for our Cartesian point of certainty. Next week, we'll start looking inside ourselves."

We do that courtesy of Sigmund Freud. His Cartesian point was sexual desire and the damage caused by our attempts to repress it. That Friday, I go to the Liberal Society disco and come on really strong to a nice-looking young man. Unfortunately for my *id*, he drinks too much and passes out before it can achieve gratification ('Serves you right,' says my *superego*). And, of course, next week the Doctor says that I was wasting my time, philosophically anyway. Like Marx, Freud created a model that repelled critical analysis: if you disagree with him, you are repressing the truth and need, not ten years in a Gulag, but more therapy.

"Freudianism's just another cult, I'm afraid," he says with a smile. "Let's go in the opposite direction, and look at science."

This isn't anyone's philosophy, but a method that has just evolved. And look at all the amazing things it has produced! Anna says something about the Atom Bomb, but she cooked me a lovely dinner the other evening and used an electric stove, not two sticks rubbed together over a pile of twigs.

But at the end of the session the Doctor reads us some 19th century material about racial types and how some are 'superior' to others, and how this is 'proven' by the 'sciences' of craniometry and anthropometrics. Then he reads us a short description of the Auschwitz Extermination Camp. Science, he says, spends a lot of time telling people what they want to, expect to, or have paid to hear.

It's nearly the end of term, now. Are we going to end up nihilists after all?

The sessions always conclude with music – Bach, Beethoven, but most beloved of all, Mozart. The *Requiem*, he says, 'has everything', so we listen to that a lot. Sometimes we also look at books on Renaissance Art or read poetry.

"You are becoming Philosophers and Lovers of Great Art," the Doctor tells us.

The rest of my time at the Poly seems pointless in comparison. Lectures, apart from Introduction to Music, are chores that I sit through. My essays are late and poor. But I don't care. Once a week, I am finding Enlightenment.

*

A few vaguely Christmassy things appear around the Poly, but as a philosopher and Lover of Great Art, I consider myself above such fripperies. The penultimate session of the Enlightenment Club is coming up, on which the Doctor has promised to reveal the route that he believes leads to philosophical truth.

The night before it, I can't sleep. I have philosophy whirring round in my head – those words: 'first cause', 'deduction', *'it must be the case that…'*, 'Cartesian point'. I see the philosophers – all men, Anna points out, but I don't care as it's their work I am interested in. If they can take away the real pain that I feel, of not knowing and needing to know, then I don't care what sex they are.

I oversleep and miss 'Modernism in Art and Design' – but I don't care. The whole day is a blur, but finally it is six fifteen and I can't be anywhere else but waiting in the corridor outside Dr Licht's office.

He lets me in early, and invites me to take a book: I pick one at random and spend a quarter of an hour learning about how, at the time of the Black Death, people walked through the streets of Europe's cities whipping each other in the hope that by driving out their own sin, they would persuade God to stop the plague.

The Doctor waits till we have all arrived – Big Ears is late – and then holds up a book with a picture on the cover of a man with a ridiculous walrus moustache.

"Friedrich Nietzsche," he says proudly, making me feel superficial (again!) about judging the author's moustache. "This man gets blamed for all sorts of things, including the rise of the Nazis. This is, of course, a calumny, as his sister outlived him and doctored his work after his death."

"I place him next to Descartes," the Doctor goes on. "Like Descartes, he was prepared to challenge all conventional certainties. Like Descartes, he ended up looking inside himself for ultimate truth – *I* think, *I* am. But Nietzsche went deeper. For him, truth was not a thing to be found but an active principle, seeking expression. It was life itself. We are drawn to it – he talked about a 'will to power', and stupid people thought he meant political power, but of course he meant the inner power that comes from living truthfully.

"That truth is subtly different in every individual human being. Nietzsche wrote: *In their heart, everyone knows well enough that they are a unique being, only once on this earth, and by no extraordinary chance will such a marvellously picturesque piece of diversity in unity as this ever be put together a second time.* That's you, Anna. And you, Stella. And you, Eustace – "

He carries on round the room, but my attention is no longer there but inside me, contemplating a unique being, only once on this earth, called Stella Tranter. The thought is shocking, freeing, terrifying.

I am not just the shy suburban nobody people take me for but *a unique being, only once on this earth.*

"So there we have it," the Doctor is saying. "Your Cartesian point is within you. You have to find it, as does everybody born to live on this earth. You can't look in the same place as other people, as there is only one you, and only one deepest inner truth, which you must seek out and then live by. 'To thine own self be true,' as Shakespeare said."

Anna is nodding enthusiastically. One of the girls is scribbling in a notebook. Big Ears is frowning.

"At the beginning of our sessions," says the Doctor, "I asked what this had to do with music, and I promised I'd answer. Now I shall. Friedrich Nietzsche was also a musician and composer, though not a very good one. Luckily for us he was an outstanding listener. He realized that a point of unshakeable, inner truth can be aesthetic, not logical or even expressible in words. It can be the experience of a moment of absolute, transcendent beauty."

A look of deep contentment steals across the Doctor's face. "That's how it was for me. I remember listening to the *Requiem* as a young man, and suddenly knowing that I had found something that I could build my life around. Something huge, solid, absolute, a glowing source of inner power that would never let me down. To me, this knowledge overcame all the arguments that bedevil the philosophies we have looked at this term – all except for Nietzsche's, of course." He pauses. "Let's listen to Wolfgang Amadeus Mozart. My truth, my Cartesian point of absolute certainty."

The speakers hiss. The first, lilting bars of the *Requiem* fill the tiny room. The voices begin to swell. Then he turns the volume down.

"Of course, that was *my* experience," he says. "What will yours be?"

Big Ears starts to speak, but the Doctor holds up a hand.

"Don't say anything now. This is just the beginning. Come and see me in twenty years time and tell me what you have found."

He fades the music back in.

*

In our last gathering we listen to music, look at more Renaissance art and read extracts from some other philosophers: Jean-Paul Sartre, GE Moore, more from

Nietzsche (who once said '*Life without music would be a mistake.*')

As I sit and soak in their wisdom, I am on the edge of tears I am so happy. Sydenham or Penge East? No, *my* station is Berlin, Hauptbahnhof. Paris, St-Germain-des-Près. Florence, whatever the railway station in Florence is called.

At the end, Anna gets to her feet and holds out a bottle of Champagne (she organized a whip-round after the last class: everyone contributed fulsomely except Big Ears, who only had 13p on him and promised to pay his part today but has now forgotten his wallet). "You've been brilliant, Stanislas," she says.

"So have you all," the Doctor replies. His eyes begin to glisten. "We could continue next term, if you wish. I'll find some time – I've a busy schedule, but where there's a will… There are many fine works of Great Art we could consider and puzzling philosophical questions we could investigate. If that would be of interest to you, of course."

"Yes, please!" we reply, virtually in unison.

*

Christmas that year is special, after all. I ask for (and get) books as presents. Nietzsche's *The Birth of Tragedy from the Spirit of Music*. Moore's *Principia Ethica* (rather hard going). *La Nausée* by Jean-Paul Sartre (even harder going: I'd wanted it in English). A book on anarchism from Lucy.

On New Year's Eve she goes to a 'happening' at someone called Sebastian's. I'm secretly hoping Anna will invite me over, but she's got involved with one of the sociology lecturers and he has invited her to a party in Greenwich. Actually, I don't mind. I have my books and I have my music. Great Art.

Mother retires early, muttering something about being another year older. "You see the New Year in for me, Stella. You're the one with the future."

I sit on the sofa and read a little of *The Birth of Tragedy*, then listen to my present to myself, a brand new recording of the *Requiem*. Our spindly-legged Radiogram with the Formica top that doesn't fit properly has never sounded so majestic, and I'm so lost in the glory of Wolfgang Amadeus Mozart that I forget to look at the clock. Suddenly it's 12.07 and 1975.

I open Anna's present to me, a bottle of dark red wine. I pour myself a glass, sniff its heady aroma and drink a toast to the Enlightened future that will now be mine.

Rebelling

Notice to all students on the Liberal Arts course. Please note that this term's lectures for Introduction to Music will be given by Professor Tyrwhitt.

The note is in my pigeonhole on the first day of the new term. Is Dr Licht OK?

Anna isn't in her usual place in the library or her usual corner in the bar. I queue for the telephone – there's a bank of five, but the coin boxes of four of them have jammed: my fellow students have been putting ring-pulls from cans into the slots designed for 2p pieces. When I finally get to the front of the queue and call her, there's no answer.

Only one thing for it. Through a couple of swing doors, up a staircase, along a gloomy corridor with peeling paint and frayed carpet. *Department of Music.* But Dr Licht's office is locked. No note on the door.

From a room marked *Departmental Secretary* comes the clatter of a typewriter. I'm nervous about interrupting grown-ups at work, but I must find out.

The Departmental Secretary is one of these immaculately neat women: cherry lipstick, bobbed hair that is as crisp as candyfloss. She turns heavily made-up eyes on me as I put my head round the door. "Can I help?"

"Yes. I... Dr Licht... Is he OK?"

"He's fine. But he's taking a sabbatical this term."

"A what?"

"A break."

"From everything?"

"From everything."

"Oh."

"Are you on the 101 course?"

"Yes."

"Professor Tyrwhitt is taking it. You should have had a note in your pigeonhole." The perfect lips break for a second into a grin: *now* will you go away.

I carry on. "I thought Dr Licht was a brilliant lecturer, and I'm really going to miss him."

"I'll tell him that. What's your name?"

"Stella. Stella Tranter. I'm… one of his philosophy students."

Suddenly the cherry lips tremble and the candyfloss looks about to disintegrate. "You lot! If you knew how much trouble you've caused!"

"Trouble?"

"With the Philosophy Department. I had that man who spits in here, raving. He said it was their job to teach philosophy; who did we think we were? As if it were *my* fault!

"They told Stanislas he had to stop his group, and he refused. So the Dean was bought in, and Stanislas still refused. Then half the Philosophy Department threatened to resign. Good riddance, in my view, but it was all too much for Stanislas and he gave in. He's now taking a term's leave of absence, and the rest of us are up to our elbows in work. It's been a nightmare."

Then she stops. The lips and the hair become solid again. "Now, if you'd kindly leave, I have a lot of work to get on with."

I nod sympathetically. "You don't have his home number, do you?"

"No."

It's a lie, I'm sure, but I don't feel up to challenging her.

*

Maybe Anna will be in the refectory. But she isn't. I get myself a bowl of chicken soup, then spot Big Ears. I feel a sudden need to be with him: he may not have been the most interactive member of the group, but he's still one of us. I go and sit opposite him, stirring the soup to cool it down a bit and feeling rather bad about the nickname, even if Anna and I just used it to each other.

"Isn't it awful?" I say.

"What?"

"About Stanislas."

He shrugs.

"You don't care?" I ask, horrified.

"Life has to go on."

His ears start to redden and suddenly I know, as surely as Descartes knew he thought therefore he was, that…

"You told them, didn't you?"

"No," he replies, but his ears are ablaze.

"You did!"

"OK, I happened to mention the matter."

"To Peabrain?"

"Doctor Pea*body* and I were having our end-of-term tutorial. I started talking about Nietzsche. He asked me where I'd learnt so much about this individual, so I told him."

"Why?"

"Because I was asked," he replies. "Dr Peabody says that irrationalist philosophers are intellectually irresponsible and can do a lot of damage. He says that those meetings were very unhealthy."

"Well, don't go to them. You sneak! You bloody little sneak!"

Big Ears scowls at me. "You're getting hysterical."

I'm not quite sure what happens next.

No. I know exactly what happens next. I pick up my soup bowl and empty it over his head.

"Sorry," I say, the moment it's done.

He sits there, immobilized with shock. I don't move either, just stand watching Polytechnic of the South Circular Student Union chicken soup oozing down the poor man's forehead.

"T - terribly sorry," I add.

A drip forms on the end of his nose, getting bigger and bigger then falls with a plop onto the table.

I reach for a serviette, but there isn't one.

I turn and run.

*

We (Anna, me and Noddy) form the Enlightenment Club Action Committee, or ECAC. The Committee has its first Meeting in the Union Bar the next day. I have a vodka beforehand to get in the mood.

The meeting goes well. We produce a slogan: *Reinstate the South Circular Poly One*. I get another vodka, and suggest we boycott Peabrain's lectures. And how about a protest march? We'll need posters, too. A clenched fist? A raised Kalashnikov?

"We'd better go and see Stanislas first," says Anna, "and ask him what he wants us to do. We don't want him losing his job."

I order a third vodka, but she's right, of course.

Anna looks the Doctor up in the phone book and rings him. He invites us round to tea. We hold a second meeting of ECAC. Our decision to accept the offer of tea is unanimous.

*

I don't remember much about our journey, except that we take a 197 bus. And that the door of the Doctor's little terraced house is blue. Then he welcomes us in with a smile, invites us to sink into some old chairs, and disappears into a kitchen. In the background, a record is playing. Bach, it has to be Bach. He reappears with mugs of tea and ginger biscuits.

"Lovely music," I say.

He nods. "Scarlatti."

Anna takes her tea. "We're furious about what's happened."

He sighs. "I'm sorry."

"You don't have to be sorry!"

"I should have played the game better. I know academic politics."

"Fascists!" says Anna.

"No, Anna, they're pompous, bullying, hypocritical and blinkered, but they're not fascists. As a young man, I watched stormtroopers marching through the streets of Vienna – and being greeted by the inhabitants. That's fascism, not a few ageing, second-rate academics pretending to act tough."

He falls silent. As do we, except for the sound of Noddy crunching on a biscuit. Then I have a bright idea. "Perhaps we could carry on our classes outside the Poly."

The Doctor shakes his head. "I had to give an undertaking not to teach any philosophy. I'm sorry, but that was part of the deal. It's not exactly easy to get jobs at my age. You are all quite right to look down on that 'saving for retirement' stuff – but the nearer retirement gets…"

Anna nods sympathetically.

"It's terribly kind of you to come here," he continues. "I really appreciate it. But I believe I have already given you the keys to being Philosophers and Lovers of Great Art."

"Find your Cartesian point!" says Anna.

"To thine own self be true!" I add.

Noddy helps himself to another biscuit.

*

I want to boycott Peabrain's lectures, but Stanislas says we ought to attend, otherwise we'll fail our exams, and what would be the point of that? At a third meeting of ECAC, it is decided by a vote of 2 (them) to 1 (me) to attend, but to sit at the back and take as few notes as possible.

The resolution is followed, but the day-glo pink biro makes no notes at all.

"That will be all," says Peabrain, squaring off his papers at the end of the lecture. Then he adds, "You'll be pleased to know, by the way, that I won't be organizing any extra-curricular musical appreciation classes."

I *can't* let that go by. I just can't.

*

The drab little office is, by Dr Licht's standards, bookless. Facing me are Dr Spigott and the Dean of Studies.

"What was it you called Dr Peabody?" asks the Dean. "In a room full of students? At the top of your voice?"

I tell them.

"Aren't you ashamed?"

I was being true to myself: Peabody *is* a pompous, bullying, blinkered old hypocrite. But suddenly I feel guilt, not pride.

"Y – yes," I reply.

"And then there's that business with Mr Crabbe and the soup," she continues. "That, surely, should give you some concern?"

"Y – yes…"

"When we admitted you to the Polytechnic, Miss Tranter, we assumed a degree of responsible behaviour. A little youthful excess is always acceptable, but there are standards of civilized debate."

I'm trying to formulate some reply involving freedom of speech, but Dr Spigott cuts in.

"I disagree. Mzz Tranter" (he speaks my appellation like an angry bee) "has a genuinely revolutionary consciousness. Anyone can sit around and have 'civilized debates'. What this Polytechnic, and this world, needs are people who take action." He grins at me. I smile weakly back.

"Like pouring soup over a fellow-student?" says the Dean.

"He was clearly a reactionary."

"And heckling a respected member of staff?"

"He's a reactionary, too."

The Dean sighs. "Hmm. Are you saying we should re-admit her?"

"Well, some sort of compromise. Start again next year. We're redesigning the course, anyway. More focus on developing a truly proletarian consciousness. Mzz Tranter is exactly the sort of student we need."

"Hmm. We've persuaded Mr Crabbe to drop the assault charges, but he may have objections to *Miss* Tranter's returning. And Dr Peabody has strong views on the bounds of academic debate." She turns to me. "Then there's the matter of your coursework, Miss Tranter. You seem to have very little interest in Liberal Arts." She sighs again. "Do you have *anything* to say for yourself?"

I try, but no words come out.

"Wise," says Dr Spigott. "Philosophers only interpret the world," he adds, giving me a knowing wink. "*Our* job is to change it."

"Hmm," the Dean says again.

*

My expulsion letter arrives a couple of days later. There is nothing about starting again next year, either.

Lucy thinks I'm ultra-cool – for a few days, anyway. Tracy Brown walks straight past me on Dartmouth Road. No loss, but I'd rather snub her than be snubbed by the stuck-up little cow. Mother seems rather happy, telling me to 'look on the bright side' and that it's time for me to get a proper job. That Liberal Arts stuff wasn't for people who want to get on with real life, was it?

*

It's a month later. I phone Anna. We can still be friends, I'm sure. We chat about people at the Poly.

"How's Henry?" I ask.

"OK. It didn't really work out."

"Sorry to hear that."

"It was mutual. I'm fine. I'm dating his partner now.

What are you doing?"

"Er, I've signed up for another college."

"Good for you. Which one?"

"Oh, it's just a small one."

"What's it called?"

"Upper Norwood."

"Ah. I didn't know there was one there. Is that part of London University? I hope they have a better philosophy department."

"Upper Norwood is more, er, vocational."

"Vocational?"

"It's... a secretarial college."

"Oh."

Silence.

"It's not just typing," I say. "I'm going to do bookkeeping, sales, principles of marketing – all sorts of stuff."

"Oh."

"I have to earn a living."

"Yes." She sighs. "Dragsville, isn't it?" Another pause. "Well, I hope I'll see you around some time."

"Of course!"

Silence.

"Look, it's good to hear from you, Stella. I've got to go now. Good luck!"

"Thanks. Bye."

"Bye."

She puts the phone down; I sit with it for a while listening to the silence and the whistling noise that follows.

Interlude 1

"We did 'how to read a balance sheet' today," I say.

"Interesting," says Mother. "How do you read a balance sheet?"

I start explaining about assets and liabilities but get confused about where debtors and creditors go.

"Interesting," Mother says again.

"We're doing more tomorrow," I add.

Constable's *Hay Wain* looks down on us from above the fireplace. Opposite it, Grandpa Scowcroft smiles cheerily beneath the military cap that he wore on 1st July 1916 when he was blown to pieces. Another grandfather, Uncle Horace's clock, tocks in the hall. There's a smell of cabbage.

Lucy is now at college studying Art, Music and Drama. She goes upstairs as soon as she can, and starts listening to her new music. It's called 'punk', and is played by Americans with ridiculous names like 'Iggy Pop'.

"What a horrible row," says Mother.

I smile, enjoying the fact that we actually agree about something. "Why don't we listen to some music, too?"

"That would be nice, Stella. But not that *Requiem* thing of yours. I find it rather morbid. How about something a bit gentler?" She starts looking through her own collection. "*Manuel and his Music of the Mountains*. How about that? So nice and relaxing."

Philosophy, Great Art and the City: Punk

I graduate from Upper Norwood in summer 1976 with a Distinction in accounts, which I discover, once I've got the debtors and creditors thing sorted out, that I'm rather good at. I start applying for jobs. At my first interview, I tell a balding man with a bright orange tie about my Distinction. He doesn't seem hugely impressed.

I know; he wants to look deeper.

"At the Poly, I was a member of a group called The Enlightenment Club," I tell him proudly. "We made a serious study of Philosophy. Descartes, Locke, Hume," (better leave out Marx) "Freud and Nietzsche."

He scratches his head and a snowfall of dandruff floats down onto his shoulders. "We don't need philosophers at Amalgamated Iron, Miss Tranter. We need people who'll roll their sleeves up and get on with it."

"We studied Great Art, too," I add, but he just scratches his head again, creating a second snowfall.

"We'll let you know," he says.

I stop mentioning Philosophy or Great Art at interviews, and soon get offered a secretarial job at a City solicitors' practice.

*

After a few months, I find a flat. My base, for my new life in the Big City. I shall not give up my passion. I shall be a Philosopher and Lover of Great Art in my spare time. London, surely, is *the* place to do this.

Meanwhile, Lucy's 'music' becomes all the rage. She joins a band and moves into a squat in Islington.

I have some special cards made, with pictures of a book and a treble clef on.

Stella Tranter
Flat 6
32 Eaglescliffe Road
LONDON W12

Lucy doesn't have any cards made.

One evening, I'm sitting in 32 Eaglescliffe reading a life of Mozart, when the phone rings. It's Lucy: do I fancy coming to a 'gig'?

I tell her I'm busy. She says there's a guy from some record company coming and they need as many people there as possible and –

"Sorry, Lucy. I really am tired."

"Selling your soul."

"Earning a living," I say pointedly: Lucy is on the dole.

Back to Wolfgang Amadeus. But I do feel a bit bad. Next day, I ring her and ask how it went.

"The bastard didn't turn up."

"Oh. I'm sorry to hear that." I mean it. I don't want her to fail. If she became a pop star I'd be delighted for her. As long as I didn't have to listen to the stuff she came up with.

"We're playing the Greyhound next Tuesday if you fancy coming along. It's just down the road from you."

"Maybe," I say.

*

I expect everyone to stare at Lucy as we board the bus at Shepherd's Bush. Her, with her Mohican, nose-stud, micro-skirt and torn stockings. But everyone seems to look at *me*.

Well, she rang up again, and sounded like she really *needed* me to come. I'll only do it once.

We get off half way down Fulham Palace Road and walk to a shabby-looking pub with torn posters outside. Tonight it's *Anne T Social and the Fuckwits*. Soon after, a dented white van pulls up and a tall, rather striking man gets out. Lucy introduces him as Jeff, 'our guitarist'. I'm not sure how a Philosopher and Lover of Great Art should greet the guitarist of the Fuckwits, so grin and say "Hi".

"Delighted," he replies, making a kind of bow. I wonder if that was genuine or taking the mickey. The latter, probably.

"Come and do something useful, Stells," says Lucy. We unload the van, lugging big wooden-boxed loudspeakers down a dingy corridor that smells of stale beer and urine. Jeff begins wiring them up onstage. I find myself watching and he starts explaining how they work. 'Pick-ups' on the guitar detect the vibration of the strings, and turn that into an electrical signal, which then goes through foot-operated pedals which enable him to alter it in various ways – he shows me some – then into a 'pre-amplifier', which... It's actually rather interesting, but at that point a bloke with earrings starts bashing a set of drums and drives me away with the racket.

I stand at the back of the auditorium and watch another guitarist set up. His guitar is hand-painted, has a sticker with *Anarchy* on it, plays the bass notes and is hideously out of tune. Then Lucy struts onto the stage and bellows into a mike.

"One... Two... Is this loud enough? BOLLOCKS!"

There's more twanging and bashing. Jeff tunes the other guitarist's instrument for him (without a tuner; he has perfect pitch). Lucy downs a pint of beer.

"Everyone ready?" Lucy finally calls out. *One Night Flop*. One, two, three, four!"

"Too fast," Jeff interrupts.

"It's punk!"

"It's still too fast. One. Two. Three. Four."

The noise that explodes from the loudspeakers is deafening. I want to rush somewhere and hide, but where?

"How did it sound?" Jeff asks me at the end.

"L – loud."

"Perfect!" says Lucy.

Jeff suggests they practice another number. Lucy tries to put him off – practicing is for old hippy musos – but they start playing anyway. The volume really is unsupportable for anyone with sensitive hearing, so I sneak off to the Ladies, where I roll up little balls of loo paper and stick them in my ears. But when I reappear, the landlord tells the band to stop as people are coming in. We go to the bar, where the drummer starts talking to me. I can't hear a word he's saying, so have to sneak off to the loo again and take the paper *out* of my ears. Then someone starts playing unpleasant pre-recorded music through the loudspeakers, again at a ridiculous level, so I have to go and get more paper...

"Upset stomach," I explain, blushing.

Once, I said. Never again.

Finally, the band goes on. Lucy struts out to centre stage, grabs the mike and shouts "'Allo" in a jubilant and totally fake Sarf London voice. Jeff starts tapping his foot and is just about to count the band in, but Lucy beats him to it at about twice the speed.

Of course, Lucy is rather good. Not musically, of course – her singing is utterly awful – but she has a kind of bizarre presence. I find talking to one person difficult enough: after about three seconds I start wondering if I'm boring them. Lucy simply assumes that everyone has come here with the sole purpose of seeing her. She grabs the attention of the entire room (which is quite full; I don't know why she was so insistent I should come) and never lets go, strutting round the stage, bellowing into the microphone, swigging beer. She fills the entire venue with her angst and her rage and her pain and her desire, and everyone (apart from me) drinks it in.

My ears start to hurt. I retire to the van and stretch out across the seats. The hideous jangle in my head slowly subsides. Before I know it, it's gone 11.00 and the audience is leaving. I head back in and help the boys dismantle the equipment while Lucy talks to the landlord. They seem to be having some sort of argument about money.

"How did it sound?" Jeff asks me again.

"OK." Then I feel bad about such dishonesty. "It was loud. Especially the singing and the bass."

To me this imbalance had been obvious, but Jeff looks at me with surprise. "I'll get Earl to turn down. If you have a word with that sister of yours, between us we'll get it better for you next time."

I nod. There won't, of course, be a next time.

Soon we have the van loaded up. Lucy turns to me. "You drive, don't you, Stella?"

"You know I do." (I passed first time.)

"Catch." A set of keys flies in my direction.

I drop them. Jeff picks them up and hands them to me. I look at him in puzzlement. "You were driving earlier…" I say.

He grins. "Somebody had to."

*

It turns out that none of them has a valid license. I can't have them getting arrested for driving around illegally, can I?

I learn to bring proper ear plugs to gigs, but still often end up sitting in the van reading or listening to music.

On one such occasion, I'm in the van when I notice someone peering in through the passenger-side window. It's Jeff. I switch the music off at once and grin at him nervously.

"Don't stop that, Stella. It's good. Mozart's *Requiem*, isn't it?"

"You… like it?"

"I did unspeakable things to one of the poor man's flute concertos when I was a lad. It was too hard for me, or I was too lazy, or I fell in love with the blues – I can't remember. I never mastered it, anyway. But I got close enough to realize how beautiful it was."

"Gosh. So how come you play…?" My voice dies.

"Punk? I love it. Aren't I allowed to love more than one kind of music?"

"Well, er, yes. Of course you are. I…"

Jeff seems to be enjoying my embarrassment. "You're a strange one, aren't you, Stella? You just roll along like a big, deep river."

"Do I?"

He starts strumming the guitar, and I recognize the song as *Moon River*. It starts as a kind of send-up, but the longer he plays, the more he gets involved with it.

"That was lovely," I say afterwards.

He looks embarrassed. "Thank you, Stella. It is rather good, isn't it, really? Henry Mancini. Not cool. But you're right." He strums one of the chords. "F sharp minor 7 flat five. Bloody beautiful."

I nod. It is.

He puts a finger to his lips. "Don't tell Earl or your sister. They'd have me thrown out for ideological impurity. They'd be totally fucked, of course – oops, pardon my language – but they'd still do it."

I smile.

Silence falls, but it's a friendly, unforced silence. "Cigarette?" asks Jeff.

"No, thanks."

"Didn't think you would."

I don't want him to think I'm completely unadventurous. "I used to. When I was a student."

"*Gauloises*?"

"How did you know?"

"Just guessed."

I feel a bit narked, but don't know what to say. Jeff starts noodling round on his guitar. I don't want the conversation to end. "I... like your guitar. It's smart. Not like Earl's tatty old thing."

His face lights up. "It's a Fender Telecaster. The greatest guitar ever made."

"Why?" I ask. A good philosopher's question.

"Wilko Johnson plays one, for starters."

"Who's he?"

"Stella, we must broaden your musical education!"

I learn all about a band called 'Dr Feelgood', and the 'machine gun' rhythm patterns used by their guitarist, Wilko Johnson, who is Jeff's rock hero and, he believes, the true father of British punk. The kinds of patterns Wilko plays are best done on the Telecaster because of the tightness of the action – that's about how close the strings are to the neck. "Here, have a feel."

"You don't mind?"

"I trust you, Stella. You're not the kind of idiot who goes round smashing musical instruments."

He hands me the guitar. I push down on a string and feel a tiny moment of wonder.

Then I hear Lucy. "We're on again, Jeff! Stop trying to get off with my sister."

"*Ein Führerbefehl*," says Jeff. "See you later."

He has a long-standing girl-friend back in Belfast, by the way.

*

Well, I'm part of the band, now, so I ought to tell you about the rest of us.

<u>1. Lucy</u> (a.k.a. Anne T Social) (vocals) (of a sort, anyway) She's attracted all the attention since she was born, so enough about her.

<u>2. Jeff Spite</u> (guitar) That's not his real name, by the way; it's McFadden. But you've met him already. And I'm still a bit annoyed he was such a smart-arse about my

Gauloises, so enough of him, too.

3. Trucker Tel (drums) Tel is the oldest member of the band. Jeff found him through an ad in Lucy's beloved *New Musical Express*. He can actually drive lorries, but got himself banned a while back – he won't say why. He also finds us most of our work, as he's played all the venues before in groups of various types: trad, pop, psychedelic, rock, funk (see: I'm picking up the terminology). "I'll play anything," he says.

He has a similar attitude to women. If anyone disappears with the girls who sometimes come backstage after our gigs, it's Tel.

"They just like me," he explains one evening. "There's not much competition, either."

"That's a little unfair," I reply.

He shrugs. "Underneath it all, Jeff is a nice Protestant boy who wants True Love and won't settle for anything less. Earl has already found his True Love, himself. You and Luce seem to be straight. So that leaves good old Tel." He chuckles, then adds, "You don't say much about your love life, do you Stella? Is there some bloke lurking in the background? I think you have a long-standing affair with a professor of Ancient Greek who plays oboe in a classical quintet. Do you write long letters to each other, on vellum notepaper?"

"I'm between relationships," I reply.

4. Earl E Death (bass) Earl is happy to admit he's not very good at playing the bass. "Music isn't about music any longer," he explains. "It's about statement. Politics. Image."

Hence, I guess, his uniform of black clothing and dark glasses. He wears the glasses even in the dingiest venues: several times I've seen him trip over pieces of equipment, despite my best attempts to keep the stage tidy. He doesn't eat properly either, with a *penchant* for fast food, which I tell him is not nutritious. Hence his sallow look. Or is it more? One day, I voice a suspicion to Lucy, that he might take drugs. She seems to find this incredibly funny.

Earl is impossible to converse with. I'm particularly bad at small talk but he thinks 'serious' conversation is meaningless. "In the contemporary world, the truly serious person is totally frivolous," he says once.

One evening, however, we're driving back down the M1 from a gig in Stafford. The other three are asleep, Jeff and Tel in the back, Lucy in the front. Earl sits between the Tranter sisters, nodding his head to some inner beat. We pass an accident on the opposite carriageway.

"Those poor people," I say – to myself really, but Earl picks up on the comment.

"They might have wanted it," he replies. "*Thanatos.* The inner impulse to self-destruction."

"I doubt it."

"But you don't know, do you, Stella?"

"No, I suppose not."

"Nobody knows what it's like to be anyone else."

I can't let that pass. "How do you know that? If you don't know what it's like to be anyone else, how do you know what anyone else knows or doesn't know?"

An ambulance, lights flashing, howls past in the opposite direction.

"You're quite clever, aren't you?" says Earl.

"I'm very clever," I reply. "I studied philosophy. It's the most interesting thing I've ever done."

"Ah... Philosophy doesn't get you anywhere, though, does it?"

"I believe it does."

"Oh, you're letting yourself down there, Stella. 'Believe' is a good word for Joe Average, but not for a philosopher. Philosophers need more than belief. They need certainty, don't they? And of course they can't have it. That's what drives them all crazy. They know they can't prove anything. All their clever arguments collapse if you push hard enough."

"That's nihilism."

"Exactly!"

"Doesn't that scare you?" I ask.

"It did for a few minutes when I first worked it out. Then I got used to it. Now I love it. It's how the world is. All fucked up and nowhere to go."

I pull out to overtake a lorry, pondering as I do so that my skill behind the wheel is not some arbitrary fact in a pointless universe but something which I have taken effort to learn and which is now proving useful to myself and to four other people too. "You really think that?"

"Of course, I do. Don't you?"

"No. I believe one can find a solid point of certainty on which to build one's life." I begin a potted version of what we learned at The Enlightenment Club.

"Great Art?" Earl cuts in half way through. "What the fuck's that? A load of old stuff touted around by middle-aged middle-class academic types. Is that at the heart of your life, Stella? Really? Honestly?"

"Yes," I say. There is, perhaps, a hint of hesitancy in my voice: I have so little time for concerts or serious reading these days.

Earl shakes his head. "You're fooling yourself, Stella. That stuff is dead — as is all the talk about 'meaning' or 'purpose'. Those are just words that scared, mediocre people make up to make themselves feel better. Whistling in the dark — and a crap tune, too."

"I don't think I could live if I really thought that."

He pauses. "No, you probably couldn't."

Then, as suddenly as he entered the conversation, he disengages. By the next junction (number 12, the A5120, which means there are 36 miles to go), he is asleep.

Philosophy, Great Art and the City: Love

I meant what I said about not having time for serious art. But one day at work Caitlin, one of the solicitors, mentions that she rehearses with a choir. Guess what piece they are working on at the moment!

"Could I come and listen?" I ask eagerly.

"You can come and sing if you want."

"Oh, no, I don't think I could do that. I can't read music."

She shrugs. "You'll pick it up. Just open and close your mouth to start with; soon you'll be singing along with the rest of us."

Caitlin is one of these optimistic, 'just go for it and it will all work out' types. Unlike, well, me. But for once I don't let 'me' put me off. I buy a score, a book on how to read music and a 'Stylophone', a toy keyboard with a picture of Rolf Harris on the packaging. Every evening I work through a section of the score, grab a meal, do another section… Twelve pages a week, I need to master.

I'm a jellyfish before my first rehearsal, but the moment the music begins I'm strong again. This is *my* music. My Mohican, my nose-stud, my Fender Telecaster.

I meet Malcolm at the second rehearsal.

It's a muggy evening; we do the *Dies Irae*; near the end, there's a judgement-day clap of thunder half way through; when we leave it's coming down in buckets. An old guy offers me a lift to the tube. I accept. We get into one of those cars with wood panelling on the outside, and talk about the piece as we inch along in a traffic jam. Wolfgang Amadeus jumps up and down in my head like the rain bouncing off the car bonnet.

Di-es ir-ae, di-es il-la.

My companion starts telling me that bits were written by a pupil of Mozart's called Francis Xavier Sussmayr, or at least finished by Sussmayr from notes Mozart left. He often tries to work out which bits are which – the *Sanctus* drags a bit so is probably not the maestro's. Of course, there is a letter dated 8 February 1800 in which Sussmayr claims to have written certain sections, but this has to be taken with a pinch of salt as he was short of money and trying to claim royalty payments on the piece, so…

We're at the tube station. He indicates to pull in and a flipper comes out of the side of the car.

"I'm Malcolm Stringer, by the way."

I fiddle in my bag and eventually find one of my

Stella Tranter
Flat 6
32 Eaglescliffe Road
LONDON W12

cards with the book and the treble clef on.

"Nice card. And nice to meet you, Stella," he continues, giving my hand a perfect shake: firm but not crushing; long enough to be sincere but not too long so as to be clingy or lecherous. Then I dash out into the rain.

At the next rehearsal, we find ourselves in the coffee queue together. Malcolm says that since our conversation he's done more research on Mozart and Francis Xavier Sussmayr, and that the experts now reckon Mozart wrote all the tunes but Sussmayr did some of the orchestration. If I listen to the *Communio* I'll find…

I suddenly feel a yawn coming on, and force my face into a series of increasingly weird expressions to prevent it, until I'm faced with a simple choice: give in or dislocate my jaw.

"You're not really interested, are you?" says Malcolm.

"No, it's just… I was up rather late last night. Working on the score," I add, in case he thinks I lead a life of unremitting hedonism.

He nods, unconvinced, and I grin back helplessly. End of friendship, I guess. Shame, I liked him.

"Would you care to have dinner with me one evening next week?" he asks.

*

"So, how was your big date?"

Well, I had to tell Lucy. It's the day after the dinner, and she is debriefing me.

"Nice."

She grimaces. "I hate that word."

"It was a lovely restaurant," I continue. "Very unassuming on the outside. Inside – class. The waiters clearly cared about the food. This guy went on about the regions of France each dish came from. The wines – "

"So it was expensive, then?"

"I guess it was."

"And what was grandpa like?"

"Don't call him that. He was very interesting. He's been to all sorts of unusual places. He's an engineer. Worked in Panama, Thailand, Arabia, Egypt – "

"Helped build the pyramids, did he?"

"Lucy, he's sixty-two. That's the prime of life for some

people."

She grimaces again.

"Anyway, older men are more interesting," I continue. "Maybe your musician friends are more fun – Jeff's rather a sweetie underneath it all – but the number of self-centred bores I've been on dates with!"

"You pick them, Stells. 'Proper grown-up doing something worthwhile', you say, then you come back complaining they just talked about lawsuits or share prices or the backstabbing at their local Conservative Party. But we're getting off the point. Tell me more about Bus Pass Boy."

"Not if you take the mickey out of him."

"Nobody says 'taking the mickey' any longer, Stells."

"I do."

She grins. "So you had this slap-up meal…"

"We had French provincial cuisine. And the conversation with it was… grown up. We talked about ourselves a bit – he actually listened to what I had to say; how's that for a man? We talked about art. Music – classical music of course. Philosophy."

Lucy grins. "Stells, he's perfect for you."

"Not really. He's married."

*

But we do keep on seeing each other. It just feels so pleasant. I tell myself we're just friends, so what's the problem? He gets precious little friendship from his wife, who doesn't share his interest in Great Art or Philosophy. They lead very different lives: she spends all her time in a 'place' they have in Hampshire, where she gardens and plays bridge with other middle-aged ladies.

Then one evening he invites me round to dinner and I find myself desperate for more than just friendship. Our eyes lock over the Quinta da Foz and Stilton; our hands seem to reach out to one another…

*

"Can he get it up?" asks Lucy when she forces the truth out of me (she says she 'can tell').

"None of your business. But, yes."

"That's something. Do you love him? Does your life divide into two parts? Part one is before you met, a rehearsal in someone's garage. Part two, after, is the live gig. Full house, crazy fucking audience, adrenalin pumping so hard you wish you could fly…"

"I'm not sure I'd put it like that. But, yes, I suppose I do."

*

Christmas is painful. No Malcolm, just family and Lucy's latest boyfriend – I can't even remember his name, but he's a music journalist of some kind – and comments from Mother about how nice he is and isn't it about time… I even have to unwrap Malcolm's present upstairs, to keep it a secret. Lucy, of course, finds out anyway and gets a fit of the giggles.

"It's a bit of old pottery!"

"It's Egyptian. From the reign of Queen Tawosaret, around 1185 BC. Malcolm found it in the desert, and had it dated."

"That's cultural theft."

"Well, maybe. But nobody else cared for it, and it was special to him. And now he's given it to me. Here, touch it. Isn't it wonderful? It makes me think of giant temples, sacred cats, women with snakey eyes, huge trumpets made from the horns of now-extinct beasts."

She runs purple-nailed fingers over it. "It makes me think of the council rubbish tip," she says.

*

I usually wait for Malcolm to contact me between what he calls our 'assignations'. He does so, regularly. We chat about art, music and philosophy but also about little things we've seen, done or felt. It feels so natural.

One week the phone doesn't ring. I tell myself there must be a good reason. We've an assignation for Saturday lunch, anyway.

On Friday evening, I'm pottering around the flat, listening to Beethoven's violin concerto. The phone rings. It'll be him!

"Er, Hello, is that Stella Tranter?"

"Yes."

"Er, I'm a friend of Malcolm Stringer's. Roy Gault."

"Oh, yes. He's spoken about you." I don't get to meet Malcolm's friends, as they all know Leticia too.

"He asked me to tell you that he's had a problem and can't make Saturday night. A family thing – he'd have contacted you himself, but he's a bit, well, busy."

"Busy?"

"His son's been in a road accident."

He doesn't really get on with his son, Colin, who's a rather wild character. "Oh," I say.

"It's nasty. Malcolm needs to spend some time with him and Leticia. He said you'd understand."

"Yes, of course," I say breezily. "Er, did he say when he'd be able to contact me?"

"He said he'd be in touch when he could. It wasn't anything important, was it?"

None of your business. "No," I say as off-handedly as I can.

*

The letter arrives a few days later.

...Suddenly realized the importance of family after all... Will always treasure the memories of our time together... Feel sure you will take this in a philosophical spirit...

I scream "No!" I rip it to shreds, try and stick the shreds together again, get Sellotape stuck to my fingers, sit in the middle of my room weeping, grab a coat, run down the stairs, pound furiously round the streets of London W12 then realize I'm lost. Luckily, a cab appears and I flag it down.

"Actually, you can stop here," I tell the driver when we get to the off-licence at the foot of Eaglescliffe Road.

Next day, I'm late for work. Mr Prendergast snaps at me and I snap back. Caitlin hears this, and comes to have a chat with me. I tell her what's happened, and she starts going on about being positive and looking for silver linings.

I call Lucy that evening, and she comes over and insists on taking me out. I suddenly want to go dancing: I don't know why, as I normally dislike disco music, but tonight I want to go crazy to it. I do, and some of the pain disappears.

Lucy hates disco, so it's sweet of her to play along. We end up back at the flat, with more – and better quality – wine, and she lets me drone on about Malcolm.

"He's only a bloke, Stells," she breaks in finally.

"He understood me."

"Well, find someone else who understands you."

"There seem to be so few people who do."

"Yes, you are a bit odd." As she says this, a chain between her nose stud and the safety-pin in her left ear rattles. "Go and get laid, anyway. It's what I always do. Get back on your horse."

"I don't have a horse to get back on to."

Lucy reaches over and gives me a big hug. "You need to toughen up, Stella. Shall I pop out and get another bottle?"

*

I go to a recital by an up-and-coming young flautist at the Wigmore Hall: after the first piece I turn to the complete stranger next to me and say, "That was so elegant, wasn't it, darling?"

Well, it's what I've got used to. I disappear at the interval, and can't face concerts after that.

Philosophy? I can't summon up the concentration. The books sit around with the markers in the same places they were a week ago, a month ago…

The only thing I've got left is the band – and they seem to be doing fewer gigs. One Saturday, they have one at the Hope and Anchor in Islington. Jeff insists everyone rehearse for it. "We've been getting sloppy," he says. Grudgingly, the rest agree, and we convene at midday.

"I've got a new song," says Jeff. He sits down, begins strumming and sings. It's rather lovely, a ballady sort of thing. Is that an F sharp minor 7 flat 5 in there? It's for Annie, of course.

"Cool singing," says Lucy. "But does it fits our – "

"It's shite," Earl cuts in.

Jeff turns and glares at him.

"Radio Two shite," Earl goes on.

"Oh, yeah. You know so much about music!"

Earl just sneers. "Middle class shite," he adds.

"Well, Earl, you certainly know all about being middle class."

This seems to hit a sore spot, especially when Jeff adds, "The complete fucking expert on that, you are."

Earl advances towards him, fists clenched. He's wearing his shades, so he trips over a lead and tumbles forward. Jeff holds out a hand to help him, but Earl appears to misinterpret this, as he grabs hold of Jeff's legs and makes him lose his balance.

Jeff topples into his speaker stack. "My guitar!" he calls out.

The Telecaster looks OK to me, but Jeff turns ice cold. Very slowly, he stands up, hands the guitar to Lucy, who's watching the proceedings with mounting interest, then rolls up his sleeves.

"You… could… have… damaged… my… guitar," he says.

Earl gets to his feet and starts to retreat. This time he treads on one of Jeff's foot-pedals and tumbles into the drum kit, which dissolves with a cacophony of crashing cymbals, sticks falling out of a holder and the thud of a floor tom-tom falling over. He grabs a now empty cymbal stand and tries to defend himself with it.

"Chaps, stop!" I say. "This isn't very nice!"

Jeff yanks the stand out of Earl's hands. "If anything's happened to my guitar…" he says, and starts prodding Earl with one end of the stand. At this point, Tel gets off his drum stool, steps across his fallen hi-hat and places himself between the combatants.

"Lads," he says. Just that.

Both look at him, then at the ground. Earl heads off to the toilet; Jeff shakes himself down and walks across to Lucy to collect the Telecaster and double-check it for damage.

The gig that evening is rather good, actually, but it's the last one that we do.

*

Lucy soon finds a new musical direction.

"I'm a New Romantic," she tells me.

"I'm an Old Romantic," I reply, remembering when Malcolm and I went to Frinton-on-Sea for a weekend.

"You must come to the Blitz Club. It's cool."

We go.

"Perhaps I was a punk after all," I say to myself as I sip an absurdly expensive cocktail. Lucy soon hooks up with a young man who looks like he's on his way to a fancy dress party dressed as a pirate. I get a cab home.

I'm late again next morning. Mr Prendergast calls me in and tells me I'm fired. I want to reply that I didn't want to work in his stupid little firm anyway. Now belatedly aware of my true punk identity, I want to tell him that the law is a middle-class plot against truth, authenticity, honesty and beauty, and, quite frankly, he can shove it up his arse.

"I'm sorry things didn't work out," I say.

*

"I'm giving notice to quit."

"That's a shame, Miss Tranter. You've been a model tenant. Is there anything we've done wrong?"

"No. I just don't want to live in Central London any longer."

"Oh dear. Last time we spoke you said what fun it was. All that culture."

"I'm fed up with culture. It hasn't helped me with my life at all."

"It's never done a lot for me. Unless you include country and western music, which I don't think you do, do you?"

"Not really."

"Going anywhere exciting?"

"Just back home."

Sydenham or Penge East?

I'll decide when I get there.

*

Lucy helps me move. The pirate is too busy to join us, or maybe he has a wooden leg and would have problems with the stairs. She hires a van with a driver, a young man who tells me proudly as he lugs another box of books into the van that he is a novelist.

"Wow," I reply. "What have you written?"

"Nothing."

Lucy has a kind of snigger she does when people say something really stupid.

"Yet," he adds quickly.

When we are loaded, I pop back up, officially to check if we've left anything behind, but actually to sit on the floor and remember what it felt like to dream of being a Philosopher and Lover of Great Art in the Big City.

Reverend, discreet, advised and sober

I'm happy.

No, really, I am. I have a lovely little flat, near Penge East station, and a job in Ladywell. Well, Lewisham, actually, but Ladywell sounds so much nicer. The Big City is a strange dream I had a long time ago. And today I'm having a clear-out of those old cardboard boxes that I never open anyway. There's a charity shop round the corner.

On the way there, I trip over an uneven paving stone and suddenly I'm sprawled on the pavement with a load of books spewed out in front of me.

"Are you OK?"

I look up to see a small, stocky man in a pair of cords and a lumberjack shirt. He holds out a hand, which I take to get myself up to my feet.

"Can I help?"

"That's most kind."

We begin picking up the books. *Discourse on Method. Principia Ethica. The Birth of Tragedy from the Spirit of Music.*

"Weren't you at Sydenham School?" he asks.

"Yes," I reply hesitantly.

"I was at the College. We did some art thing with you once." He stares up at the sky and starts flicking his finger. "Lucy. That's it. Lucy... Gotta help me out here."

"Tranter. You're mistaking me for my sister."

"Oh, right. I'm sorry. You do look alike, though."

"I'm fatter and my hair is frizzier. Though it is its natural colour: hers was probably bright green or something at the time."

"Probably. That art thing was a bit way out." He puts *A Student's Guide to Sartre* into the box. "Let me carry this... So, you still live round here?" he asks, as we approach the shop.

"Yes."

"Me too. Anything else to carry?" he adds as we walk out again.

"There's a couple of boxes of records."

"You must let me. I'm Bobby, by the way. Bobby Mowatt."

"Oh, I'm Stella. Stella Tranter, obviously. Well, no, not obviously, is it? I could have married. But I've never really... I'm not very..."

We head back to my flat, and he waits politely outside while I fetch the biggest box, which he then takes.

"Oof – that's heavy. Replacing them all with these new CD thingies?"

"Not really. I just – I don't know – went off music."

He nods thoughtfully. "Never really been my cup of tea, the classical stuff, anyway." We make the journey to the shop without incident, then hover while the assistant flicks through the records.

"Classical stuff doesn't fetch much," she says and offers me £5 for the lot. It doesn't seem nearly enough, but I'm not carrying it back to the flat.

"It was very nice of you to help," I tell Bobby when we're back out in the street.

"No problem." He looks at me with a new intensity. "You don't fancy, er, meeting up for dinner sometime, do you? On me, of course."

"Not really."

He looks hurt.

"Sorry. That sounds horrible. I don't really go out. It never seems to work and – I'm really rather happy on my own."

"Oh. Shame. Well, if you change your mind... Here's my card."

*

A few days later, I'm in the flat ironing, and suddenly think this refusing to go out is ridiculous. I rush over to my handbag and dig out the card.

Robert Mowatt
Assistant Director
Mowatt Plastics
Unit 5B
Minerva Industrial Estate
Croydon

There's a number, too.

I cross to the phone, dial most of the number, wonder what the smell is, rush across to the ironing board, shrug – they weren't very nice jeans, anyway – go back to the phone...

*

When Bobby and I meet, I make a little speech about not being much cop at 'dating' and really only looking for friendship, is that OK? He says that's fine; friendship is good. We start going to the cinema.

At Christmas, Bobby asks me to the Rotary Club annual dinner / dance. I want to look good for this, and spend a fortune on my hair and another fortune on an outfit. When I get the outfit home, I try it on again, and it suddenly looks grotesque. I contemplate returning it, but can't find the receipt, unlike a hoard of other receipts that I immediately find: for a coffee and Danish at Sam's Breakfast Bar, for a book called *Get over your Past and Live a Bright New Future*, for another coffee and Danish at Sam's.

When the evening comes, I put the outfit on and tell myself it looks OK really. My hair even looks quite good. With some nice earrings and a few touches of make-up – hell, I'm going to enjoy myself!

We arrive at seven thirty. The men look confident and powerful in dinner jackets and hand-tied bow ties, and the ladies elegant in their ball gowns. I expect to be overawed by all this, but I tell myself not to be, and it works.

We are on a table with eight other people, including someone called Bill Carr, who's some big cheese in Rotary and a few years older than Bobby, and his wife Matilda, whom I seem to recognize.

"Yes!" she says when I ask her if she was at Sydenham School. "I remember you, too. You were a bit of a rebel, weren't you? Did lots of art. Didn't you dye your hair blue once?"

I smile. "We all have our little moments of rebellion." Well, why not?

After a very pleasant dinner, a band comes on. The singer is probably the second worst vocalist I've ever heard. Never mind: Bobby orders another bottle of red.

The band finally finishes. Perhaps now we'll have some peace and quiet and be able to converse.

"Round of applause for the Sydenham Stompers. Weren't they great?"

No.

"I'm Vince Bland and I'm here to take you through to

midnight with the latest hits and some golden oldies. Any requests?"

Shutting up?

Oh, don't be such a frump, Stella. Apart from the noise level, I'm having a lovely evening.

The music starts up, and, my aesthetic defences lowered by the red, I find myself tapping my foot along to it. Then Vince puts on *Le Freak*, which I remember from my night of getting over Malcom. I glance at Bobby, who is deep in conversation with Bill about the new Labour leader, Neil Kinnock, and whether he would be any less barmy than his predecessor.

"Do you want to dance?" I ask him.

He looks paralyzed with indecision.

"Go on, Bobby," says Bill. "We're here to enjoy ourselves."

I take Bobby's hand and lead him out onto floor, and suddenly the music takes possession of me. I leap up and down, shaking my hips and waving my hair around – undoing all that money spent on it, but it feels nice. Bobby jiggles about, rather uneasily at first but with increasing energy as the song continues. In the middle bit, he starts jerking his knees from side to side and flapping his arms in the air. It's like a duck trying to climb a ladder. But it's a cute duck, an underneath-its-formal-plumage-rather-vulnerable duck.

More up-tempo numbers follow – I want to dance to them all – then the lights go down and the songs get slow. I suddenly want Bobby to hold me close, and he does. I want him to kiss me; with a little encouragement, he does. I want…

*

There are fewer people on my side of the aisle than Bobby's – Mother says that shows what a catch Bobby is. On my team, there's Mother, Mr Brown, Aunt Alice and her carer Grace, a girl called Vee who I was at Upper Norwood with, a work colleague called Tracey (I'm accountant/office manager in the travel agency in the High Street; she's one of the salespeople) and of course Lucy, with the aspiring novelist, whom she's now dating. She says marriage is 'bourgeois' but has actually been a brick, organizing all sorts of things and taking me out to get drunk one evening to celebrate 'the end of my freedom'. Father is not there: mother insisted it was impossible to contact him, and I gave in. Maybe it was even true.

"Holy matrimony is an honourable estate, instituted of God in the time of man's innocence, which is commended of Saint Paul to be honourable among all men, and therefore is not by any to be enterprised nor taken in hand unadvisedly, lightly or wantonly, but reverently, discreetly, advisedly, soberly..."

As the vicar intones those words, I feel not the end of my freedom but its beginning. A weight is slipping from around my shoulders, like that albatross in a poem we did at school. I was lousy at being a teenager and a 'young adult' (which I now realize means 'overgrown teenager'). Now I'm moving to the stage that truly matters, proper adulthood. All that other God-awful stuff was just a preparation for this: real life.

"...and in the fear of God, into which holy estate these two persons present now come to be joined. Therefore if any man can show any just cause, why they may not lawfully be joined together, let him now speak, or forever hold his peace."

Nobody will speak, of course, but we still both glance round at the congregation. I suddenly notice two men have slipped into an empty pew at the back. One is wearing a huge white collar and has long, curly hair; the other is rather Germanic-looking and has a walrus moustache. Are they about to object?

Silly question; it's just a trick of the light – the bright, fresh light that's shining in through the nave windows onto our future lives that have begun here today.

Interlude 2

I've been married six years, three months – or is it four? We have no children: I'm not sure why. Maybe neither of us wanted them enough.

Anyway, it's my 35th birthday in a just over a week's time. We have a little advance celebration, as Bobby has to be at Plastex '90 in Pittsburgh on the actual day. His mum and dad bring a bottle of Champagne; we all sit in the garden and drink it, and old Mr Mowatt says: "Big milestone, 35. Back in the old days, that was the half-way point."

"Half way point of what?" I say, rather more snappily than I'd like. Reg irritates me, though I don't really know why (which of course makes me feel bad about being irritated, which in turn makes me feel even worse.)

"Life."

I rein in a comment about not planning to die aged 70 and say, "Gosh. I hadn't thought of that."

*

The Big Day itself dawns early with a call at 4.30 in the morning. "It's what? Oh, I'm sorry – I thought it would be much later. I never get this dashed international clock stuff right… Anyway, happy birthday."

I go back to sleep and get up late – I've taken the day off. I treat myself to a bottle of Waitrose freshly-squeezed orange with my breakfast. Then I go for a long walk round the old Crystal Palace. At first I feel the simple exhilaration of being out in the fresh air, but soon this isn't enough. Half-way point or not, I want this day to be significant. I want something amazing to happen.

I get to the point where you can see the roofs of the Poly (or the University of Catford as it is now). I find myself remembering that study group – what was it called again? I see the old tape-recorder, the eager faces of the students. I can even smell those old books. Whatever happened to Anna? A strain of music comes back to me. Mozart's *Requiem*, wasn't it?

I'm right at the top of the hill now, and pause to gaze down at the sports pitches, the traffic on the South Circular Road, a train pulling out of Sydenham Hill station. Rows of houses stretch away towards the North Downs. Nice, sensible properties: ours went up by £20,000 last year.

Suddenly their sameness is horrifying. What do they do to the individual human beings who get squeezed into them? *In their heart, everyone knows they are a unique being, only once on this earth...*

Ah, yes, that quote. Nietzsche, wasn't it? An intense, hyper-critical academic who knew nothing of real life. He never married. He may never even have had sex (not that I do that much now, but you don't after a few years, do you?) I seem to remember he had a kind of Muse called Lou Andreas-Salomé, but she wouldn't sleep with him. Not surprising, with that ridiculous moustache of his.

I find myself laughing, not just at Nietzsche's moustache but at myself and my ridiculous youthful enthusiasms. Didn't I even go round in some ridiculous beret?

Time to head home and get on with the rest of my real life.

Eternal

"Alto... Some experience...." says Gloria.

"It was a while ago that I sang it," I reply. "But know the piece pretty well."

I saw the ad in the local Post Office, not long after my birthday.

> The Sydenham Songbirds
> need singers, all voices, for a performance of
> The *Requiem* by WA Mozart
> Ring Gloria on 081...

Was that some kind of spooky message up there on the common? No, I don't believe in that sort of thing. But the moment I saw the ad, something inside began nagging me.

"...And it's *Mrs* Stella Mowatt?"

"That's right."

For a while, I ignored the nagging, but it just grew more intense. 'Why not give it a try?' became 'You really ought to give it a try' and then 'So what are you afraid of?'

Gloria has a cheerful voice. "It's nice to have some other married ladies on board, Stella. We get an awful lot of unmarrieds looking for husbands and very few eligible men. You can't imagine the problems that can cause!" She laughs. "First rehearsal was last week, but if you know the piece, that shouldn't matter."

"It won't," I say.

*

We begin by practicing the *Sanctus* – not one of my

favourite bits. I find myself remembering Malcolm. That's no doubt why I make so many mistakes. As we move on to the *Benedictus* and *Agnus Dei*, I force myself to concentrate on the music.

Half way through, I realize it's not Malcolm that's putting me off, but my own complete lack of musical ability. Last time I sang I was single and had time to burn, which I spent wearing flat an old vinyl disk of the *Requiem*, poring over a score and working out every note. Now I've got a husband, a home, a life.

I'll not come again. I'm glad I accepted the challenge. It's as important to know where you don't fit as to know where you do.

"See you next week, Stella!" chirrups Gloria as we leave.

I grin. I'll give her a call during the week and let her know.

Wolfgang Amadeus Mozart, however, has other ideas. He inserts tunes into my brain at every possible moment: at work, in the garden, lying in bed waiting for Bobby to finish the Times crossword. Even shopping...

"Next, please."

Quam olim Abrahae, tiddle pom...

"Next!"

"Oh, sorry."

Promisisti...

Beep

Quam olim Abrahae, tiddle pom...

Beep

Promisisti...

The check-out lady is looking at me very strangely.

"Do you know the *Domine Jesu* from Mozart's *Requiem*?" I ask her.

"No. What is it?"

"A piece of music."

Beep.

"I don't listen to music much. There's a special offer on these. 2 for 1. Do you want to go and get an extra box?"

"Not to worry. It's really wonderful, you know."

"We like to keep customers happy."

"No. Mozart's *Requiem*. You should give it a try."

Beep.

I'm lucky, to know and love this piece. So make the bloody effort to sing it!

*

The spotlights glint off the instruments in front of us: gold off the brass, mellow off the dark wooden soundboxes of the strings, a flash of silver from the rims of the tympani. Applause breaks out as Joanna, the orchestra leader, takes her seat and as Laurence, our conductor, mounts the podium. He gives a flourishing bow, turns, taps his baton twice on his music stand and raises it. The music begins. Slow and stealthy. Then it's two bars till our entry. Then one bar…

I've practiced so hard for this – but I suddenly know it's all going to go wrong. I'll come in a beat early, and when I do so a hideous braying noise will emerge. Everyone will turn and stare in horror.

We all come in together, right time, right note, as sweet as can be. Our voices build slowly up through the *Introit* into the *Kyrie Eleison*. The music grows with us, expanding, like one of those speeded-up films of flowers opening leaf after leaf, welcoming life. Then the *Dies Irae*, and a new metaphor comes unbidden to me. I'm with a mysterious man in a strange place. He walks up to me and kisses me. We begin ripping the clothes off each other, and –

Stella! We're in a church! This is Mozart!

Luckily, the next section begins with just a trombone and a soloist, and my imagination is reined back. As the other soloists enter and begin to trade exquisite melodies, I'm not reminded of anything erotic or even floral. It's rather a relief.

The music flows on: the anguish of *Lacrimosa*; the sudden restless energy of *Domine Jesu*; the gentle *Benedictus*; the triumphal final ascent to *Lux Aeterna* – light eternal. We mount a golden, angel-lined staircase, with huge rococo doors at the top which fly open on the final D chord, which Laurence holds and holds till our lungs are fit to burst with joy.

Applause is echoing round the building. I want to hug and kiss the singers all around me. We are ordinary people, but together, tonight we have created something truly transcendent.

*

"You looked like you were enjoying yourself," says Bobby as we drive home.

"Oh, yes! It was like… Well, it's hard to say what it was like. How about you?"

"Yeah. You know it's not really my thing, classical music, but I didn't get bored. Well, not much."

"Not much?"

"The solo sections were a bit long. But when you lot were letting rip – it sounded good." We join a queue of cars. "These lights! They only let about five cars through at a time. We're on the South Circular, for heaven's sake, not some B-road. Europe's other capital cities have proper traffic management systems!"

We don't really talk about the concert after that.

*

We get an excellent write-up in the Gazette. I buy a scrapbook and glue the review in next to a flier and Bobby's programme and ticket, which I rescued from the waste paper bin. I ponder what transcendent music will fill the rest of the pages.

A few weeks later, a letter comes: we've been asked to repeat the performance at St Ethelbert's church, Ingelow, as part of a music festival. There's no money. Ingelow is up on the East Coast somewhere, so it will be quite a journey there and back. The orchestra is made up of local amateurs, and may not be much good. Would I be interested?

Of course!

I suggest to Bobby we make a weekend of it.

"You go and have a sing," he says. There's a slightly derogatory tone to his voice – or is that just my imagination? "I'll stay here and get some serious golf in."

*

"As far as we know, St Ethelbert's was commenced in 1317. You can still see traces of Early English in the north aisle."

I'm trapped.

"The transept windows take the simpler lancet form, which soon evolved into the more sophisticated arches of the Decorated period."

Helplessly trapped.

"Then along came the Black Death, which put a stop to church building for a long time. A blessing in disguise, of course, as church architecture had evolved considerably by the time building was recommenced."

I nod. A disease so horrific that it killed half the population and drove people to self-flagellating mania, but it got this old bore's church window looking nicer, so that was OK. I wonder if I could get a tiny bacillus and drop it in his wine.

You're not being nice, Stella. You're a guest. Be nice.

We came up on the coach today and have already had a sing-through in the church where we'll be performing tomorrow. It sounded a bit rough, but we have the day to sort things out. We're now at a reception in someone's house.

"Of course the actual glass is undistinguished. Cromwell destroyed the original with his usual thoroughness, and the Victorian replacements lack originality. The apse is of similar mediocrity. The rood-screen – "

"Hello, George." A new person joins our twosome. "Good to meet you again, Stella," he adds.

"Oh, gosh. Nice to see you too."

My rescuer is one of a group who met our coach when it arrived in Ingelow's market square. Of course I've forgotten his name.

"Alex," he says, noticing my indecision and holding out a hand. "Settled in?"

"Yes."

"And you've had a walk round the town? You should. Be a bit careful, though. The centre is lovely, but there are some quite rough bits just beyond it. A dark heart beneath a smiling exterior, that's Ingelow. Wouldn't you agree, George? George? Oh dear. I seem to have driven him away. I'm terribly sorry."

"No need to apologise. He was rather a bore, actually."

Oh, God, what have I said?

Alex just smiles. "Can I get you a drink?"

While he refills my glass with Champagne, I study a poster hanging nearby. The Ingelow Festival presents Bach's *Mass in B minor*. The Ingleside Singers. The Fenland Orchestra (leader, Alex Collings).

"Is that you?"

"It is, actually. Cheers." He raises his glass and I do the same. They chink, and I hold mine up to a light and watch the little pearls of nothingness appear from nowhere then bubble joyfully up to the surface.

*

Morning rehearsal. My head is not at its best. Nor is the orchestra, perhaps because its leader is missing.

Oh, God. Alex had an accident on the way home after the party (he said he lived out of town). We had several glasses of fizz together after our first one: he was so charming. And now he's wrapped his car round a tree and died in slow agony *and it's all my fault*.

Bobby says I do this – jump to 'irrationally excessive conclusions'. Concentrate on your singing, Stella.

"*Kyr* – oops, sorry. Bar too early!"

Actually, we're *all* rubbish, not just me. Roll on lunchtime.

Roll? We get bread, curly white bread with marg and paste made out of some low form of aquatic life. I wander outside, watch the citizens of Ingelow going about their Saturday afternoon business and envy them: they're not in the middle of destroying a great piece of music.

"Back to work, people." It's Laurence. "*Confutandis Maledictis*, from the top!"

That's the section where I mess up the most. Oh, well, it's only a weekend… I hope Bobby is having more fun with his golf.

Alex has arrived, and is tuning up.

I want to rush over and give him a hug and say how pleased I am that he didn't die in a car accident night. But that might seem a bit odd.

The strings re-tune to him. When they are ready, he nods to Laurence, who counts us in. The orchestra sounds ten times better already. This in turn lifts the singing. This morning's *Requiem* was a wounded eagle that had been desperately flapping its wings in a failed attempt to fly. Now it has found a thermal that is sending it soaring skywards with the natural majesty for which it was created.

When the rehearsal is over, I hang around, hoping to speak to Alex again. I'm not sure what I want to say – nothing about cars and trees – but he seemed good at creating conversation, so maybe my lack of ability in that department won't matter. But he's talking to Laurence anyway. So I tag along with a group of fellow Songbirds heading back to the hotel. I need go get myself mentally prepared for tonight.

It will be special, I tell myself.

Taking a Chance

It is.

Wolfgang Amadeus Mozart and the Sydenham Songbirds have done it again.

Applause is ringing round the rafters of this magnificent (despite the Victorian glass and whatever was mediocre about the apse and the rood screen) church. Laurence takes yet another bow, then turns and gestures to us a third time.

"I'm off to the pub," says one of the basses, as the applause begins to die down and people start getting up from the rather uncomfortable pews where they have been sitting. "There's one round the corner. Anyone coming?"

"Sounds good," says Gloria. "Stella?"

"Yes. I'll… be along in a minute." I stand and tinker with my folder, still reeling with the elation of having co-created something so completely beautiful, then turn to watch Alex packing away.

I summon up courage and walk over to him.

"Hi…"

"Oh, hello, Stella. Didn't we do well?"

We. The orchestra leader talking to one rather unmusical member of the choir. "Yes!"

"Some of us are going for a drink," he goes on. "The Bakers' Arms. You get a better pint there than that God-awful plastic place round the corner. Want to join us?"

*

'Us' turns out to be just Alex, me and a group of brass players who are soon involved in a drinking contest. We find a more discreet alcove. Alex tells me about his time as a music student, playing in a provincial orchestra for a bit, how he now earns a living from teaching. "Private pupils, plus a couple of days a week at King Ethelred's – that's the posh school in town. Not that anything's really posh in Ingelow." Then he asks me to tell him something about myself.

"I'm a philosopher," I say.

Where did that come from?

Alex looks impressed.

"Well, I did it at uni," I add hastily. "Polytechnic, actually."

He doesn't seem concerned about the grade of my educational establishment. "I regard myself as a philosopher, too," he says instead. "Are you familiar with Nietzsche's *The Birth of Tragedy from the Spirit of Music*?"

"Familiar? I loved it!" I say, then try desperately to remember what it was about. "Apollo and Dionysus. The union of pure classical beauty and the energy of the life force."

"The Artist, especially the Composer, as a priest of the transcendent in a vulgar world," he replies with a nod.

"The alienation of humanity from its natural roots!" I add, and suddenly I'm talking about Dr Stanislas Licht and the Enlightenment Club in a way that I haven't done to anyone since Malcolm. As I do so, the thrill of those sessions in that cramped little room comes back to me. The piano, the sheet music, the bust of WA Mozart, the tape recorder, the books, the sense of adventure, of change, of possibility.

A jukebox in one corner, which has been silent up till

now, suddenly starts playing *Take a Chance on Me*.

Alex's face falls. "I write proper music," he says.

I nod. I quite like Abba, but sitting here now – well, it is a bit whiny, isn't it?

"I'm working on a concerto," he goes on. "I have been for a while – the birth pangs are proving hard on this one. Would you like to hear it? As far as I've got, anyway."

"I'd love to."

"Come on. Drink up."

As we get up to leave, the brass players give a raucous cheer, presumably something to do with their drinking game.

*

The church door creaks open. Alex finds the lights: the sound of the switches booms round the nave, as do our footsteps and the plop of him putting his violin case down on a pew. He gets out the instrument – there is such delicacy in how he holds it and nestles it into his body.

"May I present the first movement of the violin concerto in E, by Alex Collings!"

La, laaaaaa, la, la, laaaaaaaa. Da, da, da, da, da, da.

The door creaks again. "Hello?"

"Fuck," says Alex. The word also echoes round the nave.

"Oh, Mr Collings, it's you."

"Yes, Joe."

"I thought you lot had all gone. I've got to lock the church up now."

"Can we have another ten minutes?"

"Sorry. It's later than the vicar agreed anyway."

"Ten minutes. This is important."

"Locked up at ten o'clock, Mr Johnstone said."

"Bloody philistine," Alex mutters. A look of sudden, intense fury crosses his face. Then he seems to rein it in; maybe it's putting the violin back in its lining that has this calming effect. "We could go back to my place and I'll play it for you there, if you like," he says.

*

There's a grand piano in the middle of Alex's big, main room; the walls are covered with posters of concerts, and there are plenty of bookshelves. He gets out the violin, tunes up – then suggests we have drink first. Glass of wine? Well, why not? We sit on a big sinky sofa and talk.

"You're a real inspiration, Stella."

"That's very kind of you."

"No, I mean it. You make me feel... free, somehow. To create. To make art. To take on my demons."

"Demons?"

"Laziness. Mediocrity. Inauthenticity. Our friend Nietzsche understood this so well. If we aren't true to ourselves, who can we be true to?"

"No..."

He sighs. "I've spent so much of my life living untruthfully, Stella. And the reward? Just enough money in the bank. Some souvenirs." He gestures round the room.

"They look nice."

"I want more than nice, Stella. I want true. Beautiful. Inspired. Those satisfactions come from great Art, and nothing else..." He pauses. A frown crosses his face, just briefly, then he cheers up. "Let's have some more wine!"

Various voices tell me to refuse. "Let's," I say.

As he heads off to the kitchen, I know I belong here,

with the piano, the posters of concerts, the books, doing whatever I can to help this man make Great Art.

Right

"Anyone at home?"

"Yes. Hello Bobby!"

"Had a good time?"

"Yes. We were fantastic, and the punters loved it!"

"Punters?"

It's an Alex word. A 'muso' word.

"Audience," I say. The clubs clank as he puts them next to the elephant's foot umbrella-stand. "Good round?" I ask.

"Oh, the usual ups and downs. I played a great shot at the 14th. Must have been a hundred and fifty yards and ended up six feet from the hole. Of course, I then three-putted. Crazy game!"

"Maybe I ought to learn, so we could play together."

"If you don't mind being driven mad."

"I'm mad already," I say flippantly, then cross over to him and put my arms round him. He is a little surprised and makes a gesture half way between a squeeze and a flinch.

"It's nice to see you," I say, feeling an explanation for my action is needed. "Fancy a tea?"

I go into the kitchen and turn on the kettle: silent at first, it begins to gurgle, then to jiggle about with a kind of insane, dancer's joy, belching steam. Then it gives a click and falls silent.

As I plop the bags into two mugs (*Plastex '87, Milwaukee* and *Plastex '89, Stuttgart*), I tell myself that the best thing to do is to be upfront and tell him now. Everything.

I take the tea through. "There's something…"

Bobby looks up at me.

"…wonderful about a cup of tea after a long journey, isn't there?" I go on.

*

I ought to tell *you* what happened, though, shouldn't I?

Alex came back from the kitchen with the bottle, and we drank a toast to Art, and talked more about music – well, he did most of the talking – and then he suddenly broke off and looked terribly sad. "I've not lived up to my dreams," he said, and I said "Not yet", and he took me by the hand and said how he needed my inspiration. I knew two things as he said that; one that I should terminate the conversation at once, and two that it was completely impossible for me to do so. Instead I leant forward and kissed him.

I'm not proud of that, and even less proud about what happened after that.

But it was bloody wonderful.

*

On the train in to work, I rootle in my bag and find the card he gave me.

Alex Collings
Musician, Composer
26 Common Road
Cawston
Ingelow
AT29 8QX

When I get to Blackfriars, I'll find a bin and drop it in there. It was bloody wonderful, but now it's back to real life. I've got my memories.

When I get there, I can't find a bin.

At work, I wait till nobody else is around, then take the card out again.

Alex Collings
Musician, Composer
26 Common Road
Cawston
Ingelow
AT29 8QX

There's a bin here, but people might look in it and ask questions. I'll find some other way of getting rid of it.

Tomorrow.

Maybe.

*

I become two people. Old Stella is unaffected by the trip to Ingelow and gets on with things exactly as before. New Stella is bright-hearted and young again – no, young for the first time, as when she was actually young, she was always struggling (except, perhaps, in that tiny room full of books and tapes and philosophy and WA Mozart). New Stella is bubbly, optimistic, everyone's friend. And living a lie, of course.

Naturally these two Stellas can't stand one another. 'Where are you taking me?' the Old one asks the New.

'To my true self,' New answers back.

'I don't know what you're talking about!'

'No, you don't, do you?'

A third Stella, Sensible, moderate, come-on-everyone-let's-sort-this-out Stella, steps in. She reminds Old that New isn't totally new. Remember that picnic in Dulwich Park? When the daffs were out? That sudden feeling of total joyousness, just to be alive…

'I was six,' New Stella snaps back.

*

One evening, Bobby's out at a Chamber of Commerce meeting and all the Stellas are sitting at home. They are reading a book on existentialism. New saw it in a second-hand shop the other day. Old disapproved, of course, but New insisted. They have come to a bit about the importance of action.

I must *do* something.

Like what?

A letter is best. Things can go wrong on telephones.

Dear Alex…

'No, this is all wrong,' says Old Stella.

'Be true to yourself!' New replies.

Even Sensible, moderate, come-on-everyone-let's-sort-this-out Stella reckons that anything is better than this impasse. Seeing Alex again might solve the whole thing. He'll suddenly look ridiculously false and provincial, or he'll let slip some unpleasant thing about his past – and suddenly this infatuation (all of us know that's what it is) will be over.

New scribbles *that* address on the envelope and heads off to the postbox, where she balances the letter on the lip of the slot then flips it in with the kind of flip a free-spirited existentialist philosopher would give when posting a letter to one of her many passionate and exotic lovers.

Old watches, helpless.

*

One o'clock, we said, didn't we? I treble-check the name of the restaurant Alex suggested, then look up at the clock again.

He's not coming.

I stare into the glass of fizzy water that I ordered. The bubbles appear, make their brief journey to the top then, pop, they are gone. Not much of a life, being a bubble.

'This is for the best,' says Old Stella.

New keeps staring at the bubbles.

"Stella!"

"Alex!"

"I'm sorry. The train…" He looks even finer than he did in Ingelow. He stretches out his artist's hand, strong but gentle, formed by the creation of Cartesian points of beauty. I hold out my accountant / office manager's hand; he takes it anyway, then steps closer and makes to put his artist's arms around me. I back off, then feel ashamed of this bashfulness and let him hug me. Then we kiss on the cheek, then retreat to our places across the table.

"So – how's the music?" I begin.

"I'm still a bit stuck with the concerto, but… I've been doing a lot more playing since you got back in touch."

"That's great."

"We're doing a concert in a couple of months. Nothing adventurous, I'm afraid. I'd love you to come and listen. You're always welcome to stay over," he adds mischievously.

The waiter reappears. "What would madam like?"

To go to Alex's concert and stay over. "Vegetable lasagna, please."

"Would madam like wine?"

"No, I'd – better not."

"Have half a glass, at least," says Alex. "I'm sure Nietzsche would have done."

"Well, OK then. But that's all."

*

"Shall I order another bottle?"

"No, I must do *some* work this afternoon."

"Coffee, though?"

"Oh, yes."

The coffee means another quarter of an hour bought. Another quarter of an hour of music, philosophy, Apollo, Dion – whatever he's called… But of course, it ends, as it has to. Alex insists on paying the bill and we walk slowly towards the tube station.

"So…" Alex says.

"It's… difficult," I reply.

"Life's difficult. That is why Art is."

We share a proper kiss by the great big Underground symbol, then I have to go. I trudge back to work, but in my heart I am on the tube, then on the 15.25 to Ingelow, and then on the road back to Cawston and 26 Common Road and that sofa and…

Holy Matrimony is not by any to be enterprised nor taken in hand unadvisedly, lightly or wantonly, but reverently, discreetly, advisedly, soberly.

What am I doing?

*

When Bobby comes back that evening, I hold him for a long, long time.

"Are you OK?" he asks.

"Yes… I'm fine." He doesn't look convinced. "Bad day at work," I add.

"Smells like you had rather a good day."

"Oh, yes, well – that was the problem. A couple of the

girls and I went out and had a bottle of wine, and Trevor got all ratty about it."

"I can see his point of view. Productivity losses due to excessively long lunches cost the economy billions of… Ah, but everyone needs to celebrate from time to time. Any special reason?"

"One of the temps was leaving." The lie is horrible, but telling it is frighteningly easy.

We talk idly over the dinner, then Bobby says he's turning in early. He's got 'a bit of a day' tomorrow.

"I'll join you," I say cheerfully.

"Good idea," he says, though he doesn't sound hugely excited. In bed, he gives me a peck, rolls over and nods off, leaving me alone with my thoughts. *Reverently, discreetly, advisedly, soberly*, I remind myself.

Then suddenly Alex and I are on that sofa, making love.

*

I wander downstairs next morning and pick up the *Times* from the doormat. I wonder what paper Alex reads. The *Guardian* probably. Or maybe he despises all media for their inauthenticity. I make a mug of tea – *Plastex '83, Chicago* – and curl up on the sofa, cradling the drink in my hands. Bobby appears a few minutes later. At the same moment, post clanks in through the letterbox. Bobby wanders over to it, as if he expected its arrival to coincide with his, and begins sorting through it.

"I can't stand it any longer!" I exclaim suddenly.

"I know. The amount of junk mail one gets these days."

"No I mean my life. Our life. Here…"

"Oh. What's wrong?"

"I don't know," I lie, suddenly horrified at my outburst. Is there a time machine I could borrow, so I could pop back thirty seconds? That's all I'd need...

"Hmph!" says Bobby. "Can we talk about this later? Have a think. Get some things down on paper. A list we can go through and sort out."

"A list?"

"First step in problem-solving: specify the issues. If you draw up a list, we can sort it all out."

*

"Done that list?" he says that evening.

"No."

"Oh. Why not?"

"I don't know," I say, ashamed to admit I've got through half a notepad, then, half an hour ago, started flushing the scrunched up bits of paper down the loo, realized that wouldn't work, taken them into the garden and, after triple-checking that nobody was looking, set light to them, then cleared up the ashes with a dustpan and brush and mixed them in with other stuff in the black dustbin. Even this, I know, isn't perfect: I've seen things on the TV where the police can take charred paper and find out what was on them.

"Stella, you've got to be more proactive."

"I... know."

"So what's the problem?"

"I... need to be myself."

"Oh... But... you are yourself, aren't you? Who else could you be?"

"I don't know. Nobody?"

"That doesn't make sense. Everybody's somebody. Nobody's nobody. Well, I suppose that's obvious really." He pauses. "I don't really understand this 'being yourself' stuff. We're just... who we are. Aren't we? I really think you need to make a list. Come up with some specific action points."

Silence falls.

This is, of course, ridiculous.

"Bobby, I've met someone else."

He stares at me for what seems like forever, then turns away. I stare at the back of his head, appalled at what I've just said but at the same time overcome with relief. For a moment I want him to swing round and erupt with fury: the alpha male furiously defending what is his.

He turns round slowly. "Oh," he says.

Silence falls again.

"He's called Alex Collings," I blurt out. "He's a musician. He's..." Then I can't think of anything to say.

"I'm not very musical, am I?"

"No. But it's not just that."

"Oh. What is it, then? No, don't say. I don't want to know." Another long pause. "We'd better *both* do a list, Stella," he says.

*

- I'll write to Alex, wishing him well but saying I shan't be in touch again.
- Bobby and I will talk more.
- We will make love at least once a week.
- I'll give up the choir.

(Bobby recommended the bullet points.)

Well, what else can I do? I made a promise in that

church, and I must keep it.

"God is dead," mutters a Germanic-sounding voice.

*

I hoped the pain would abate. But it seems to get worse.

Several months later, I'm walking past the old Poly. Articulated trucks are, as usual, thundering by a few feet from my face.

Go on, says a voice in my head.

Go on what?

You know you want to.

Want to what?

Finish the whole bloody charade. Here's God knows how many tons of metal travelling way in excess of 30 mph. Just step out in front of it and the pretence will be all over.

No!

Yes! Authenticity, that's what life is for. If you can't live that way, you're just a fake, a non-person, nothing, a phoney, a coward. *Salaud*, that's what Jean-Paul Sartre would call you.

Huh! It's all right for him. He was a writer. He was a professional philosopher. He was French. I'm an accountant / office manager from South London.

The next articulated lorry barrels past.

Salaud! says the accusing voice.

Carlo's Café has been replaced by a trendy bistrot (I stopped going to Carlo's ages ago, and one day it was just boarded up; I never even got to say goodbye to Carlo). I hurry in and find the remotest seat, where I order a mug of lightly-scented hot water, alias 'bergamot and mandarin tzigane'. It costs as much as a full plate of bangers, eggs and chips plus unlimited refills of dark brown tea did at Carlo's.

"I'm doing what's right," I tell myself. "Right!"

People turn and give me funny looks. Another truck passes and makes little ripples in the drink.

*

I hand in my notice that afternoon, asking to leave at the end of the week. I call Lucy, and arrange to stay at hers for a bit. Then I go back to the house and pack. What things do I want? Very few.

I leave a note.

Everything you do is by the rules… Philosophy and Great Art mean nothing to you… Despite your ridiculous 'list', things haven't changed because you can't change.

Well, I write it, re-read it (several times), edit it a bit – put in a bit more venom! – edit it a lot – maybe that was bit below the belt – then shove it down the sink disposal unit, which takes ages to chew it up. Clearly the unit finds self-serving cruelty indigestible.

I write another note. *I'm just going away for a few days… Nothing to worry about…*

The sink unit dislikes lies, too.

I get writing again.

Dear Bobby,

This is written in great turmoil and great sadness. I've tried desperately to make things work, but over the last months I have felt more and more a stranger in our own home, in my own self, even. I can't stand it any longer, and don't know what to do other than leave.

You are a decent man, and deserve better than this: the fault is mine, but in the end, that doesn't change things. I wish it did.

It would be wrong of me to string you along, saying that 'one day

I might come back'. I don't know what the future holds, but I must set out without promises I cannot guarantee to keep.

You have things to support you that I do not have – friends (it's true, all 'our' friends are his), *your work, a faith* (I seem to have lost mine, or maybe I never actually had one, just the pretence of one to make life look easy). *These are deserved – you are a better person than I am. I beg you to use them and find real happiness.*

I am so terribly sorry about this.
  With affection and enormous regret
    Stella

I consider putting this down the unit too, just to see what it thinks of this version. But I must trust my own judgement. I add a PS, that I'm going to Lucy's for a bit, then reread the note. Maybe I should take out that line about –

No. Just go.

Wonderful

A mechanical female voice reads off the list of the remaining stations: Little Groaning, Podsworth, Ingelow. I imagine her: a cartoon robot with a blonde wig on. I look round at the other passengers (the train got a lot emptier after Cambridge) and wonder if any of them are making life-changing journeys, too. They all look rather bored.

It feels a lifetime ago that I left Bobby. Lucy has been bloody marvellous, listening to me talk, talk, talk and only occasionally telling me I should have done this years ago. She also said that I should contact Alex a.s.a.b.p. However, some sense of propriety stopped me. Just rushing off into the arms of someone else seemed vulgar. Lucy shrugged when I said this, and asked me how long I wanted to punish myself for.

Bobby and I talked, of course. His moods varied, and I wished with all my heart that the hurt ones would go away, but I know they wouldn't and won't.

"I expect you'll be after me for half the house," he said at one point, and I replied no, I hated the thought of him being turfed out of his home or racking up some huge debt to buy me out. "All I want is to be me," I said.

"What the fuck do you mean by that?" he snapped back, and I replied that I didn't know, but it was what I wanted.

One evening, MC Lucy-fer (that's her new incarnation) was out doing a gig. I sat and stared at the phone, then began dialing Alex's number.

Now here I am, invited for the weekend.

The robot – for some reason, I've named her Caroline – informs me that our next 'station stop' will be Ingelow. The train begins to slow down. Then we are here! The doors whoosh open. I gather my things and step out into a salt-sharp wind.

Alex is standing at the other end of the platform. He breaks into a huge grin as he spots me. I break into a run. When we meet, there's a moment when we just look at each other, then we are in each others' arms. We kiss, tentatively at first, then ravenously. I jolt to life (just as Caroline must have, when her creator first attached the electrodes).

When we stop, the platform is empty.

He takes my case in one hand – it's light; I'm travelling without baggage in every way. With his other hand, he takes mine in a firm grip, and we walk out to his car. Inside, we share another kiss, then drive off, past plain brick houses and take-aways, which look cheap and probably unhygienic but oddly exotic. I want to eat at the Peking Garden!

We don't say much. We don't need to. Soon we're out in the flat-looking countryside, then in a village, then crunching across gravel.

I want him to pick me up and carry me over the threshold, but he fiddles with the front door key then does a kind of ushering-me-in gesture. "Do you want a coffee or something?" he asks.

"I want to make love with you," I say, brazen, beautiful and, yes!, me.

*

He has a small bottle of Champagne in the bedside cabinet, which we drink sitting up in bed. I hold my glass to the light of the window and do my bubble-watching thing, though I now know the bubbles are joyous. If you must have a short existence that ends with a pop, do so exuberantly, with passion! I want to tell my lover how utterly wonderful it felt doing what we have just done – even though I wish I hadn't yelled an obscene request at one moment. But I can't find the words.

So we just drink, then touch each other again, then simultaneously decide to get up and wander back down to the big main room, where I sink into the sofa and stare at the fireplace by which we are going to spend long evenings talking Music and Philosophy and the Nature of Art, and every now and then make love (maybe with *Dies Irae* on the stereo at full volume). Alex rustles up a meal: at one point I pad across the floor – earthy old flagstones, covered in places by an assortment of rugs – to see if he needs help. He gives me a squeeze and says it's nearly ready: I get some plates out then just sit and look at him doling out pasta and supermarket meat sauce and know this is going to be the most delicious meal I've ever tasted. After it, we snuggle on the sofa. A furry black cat, which Alex introduces as Liszt (Brahms, he tells me, got run over a couple of years back), appears and settles onto my lap.

"Now!" he says suddenly. "Now's the time for me to play you my concerto."

"Yes, please!"

"It's not actually finished – but I've made progress. I did some writing today that felt really good."

"Brilliant."

The fiddle is sitting on the piano. He picks it up, with such love, and tunes it.

"Right," he says. "Music for my Muse."

La, laaaaaa, la, la, laaaaaaaa. Da, da, da, da, da, da…

The cat screeches, digs his claws into my thighs and flees into the kitchen.

Alex stops. "Damn. Sorry about that. Start again…" He tucks the violin under his chin, raises the bow, then shakes his head. "The moment… It's gone. I'll play it tomorrow."

He starts putting the fiddle into its case, then pauses. We both have the same idea at the same time. "Here, hold it," he says.

The violin is lighter than I expected. It feels extraordinarily delicate, but also powerful and alive. It is the Spirit of Art.

"Bach!" Alex exclaims. "We should listen to Bach."

We do, then it's bed again. Our lovemaking is inspired by the music we have just heard; it is slow and intricate and incredibly deep. Then cuddles and sleep – for Alex, anyway. I lie awake, wondering what I have done to deserve this. I run my hands over his face and chest, then lie back listening to his slow, steady breathing.

Find one point of absolute certainty, then build on it.

*

Next morning, Alex says he must really rehearse the concerto before playing it to me. I say that's fine; I'll have a wander round the village. Cawston has low cottages made from dark stone, a green (or at least a triangle of grass), a pub (the Crusoe Arms), and a church made of the local red stone. I hesitate at the gate of the churchyard – is it really authentic for a Nietzschean to go in and have a nose?

A Nietzschean can go anywhere, do anything!

The church turns out to be locked. As I walk back

down the path, I read the names on the graves and wonder which of these people found true love in their lives and which of them had to make do with second best.

When I get back, the concerto is still not quite ready. No problem. Alex plays me some stuff on the piano, then it's time for the Crusoe Arms. We get drunk, which is delicious.

"To art and alcohol!" says Alex, raising his final glass. "The two things that make life worth living!"

"And love," I add.

He grins. "Yes, of course. And love!"

He looks me in the eye and we clink glasses.

On Sunday morning... Well, let's not go into that. But in the afternoon we go for a long walk on Ingelow North Beach, which is only about two miles away (I *thought* I could hear the sea the day before). There are gaggles of tourists for bit, then just sand, shells, wind, clumps of bladderwrack, the occasional gull – and me and my Artist. And the sea itself, of course, still distant. Alex says that when the tide comes in it's so fast that walkers can be outpaced by it. People have drowned here: their own stupid fault, of course, but one needs to be careful.

I glance out at the thin white line on the horizon and will it to come roaring in, as I have an affinity with everything wild and powerful.

Terrible

I head back to London very early Monday morning, on a special train for zombies, but it seems pointless being there. Ingelow is where I have to be.

I hand in my notice at the agency. They say I can leave at the end of the week: I feel a little insulted but also delighted.

So at the end of that week I'm heading up to my new home and checking into a B and B on London Road. It's spartan but it's cheap. It's only going to be temporary, I know. I get a copy of the Ingelow Trumpet on Saturday morning, and by mid-afternoon Monday I have a job as accountant / office manager for Zzapp! Marketing (I tell myself I'll find something more suitable for the Muse of an Artist later; this will do for now), starting straight away.

"We have a Positive Attitude here," says Stuart, my new boss, as he shows me into my office.

"Suits me," I reply.

"Your thoughts make you who you are," he continues. "Think Positive, Be Positive."

"That's me!" I say.

I spend a lot of time at Alex's, and find myself doing more and more about this wonderful, music-filled house. Lucy would give me a lecture at this point, but the place is a bit of a mess, I feel good sorting that out and Alex appreciates it. Stuart would call that a Win/Win Outcome. Soon, it makes obvious sense that I move in. When I suggest it, he's not as happy as I hoped he'd be, but he sees the logic of it.

"We philosophers are logical," I say.

Nietzsche, he points out, disliked logic, and we have a little debate about that. Dr Licht always said that Nietzsche was fiercely logical in his own way. Alex says that for him, one of the joys of Nietzsche was his dethronement of logic and its replacement with Art as the central human experience.

I suspect we're saying the same thing, really, but just in slightly different ways.

I still haven't heard the concerto. After a brief burst of creativity, Alex got stuck again, and he really wants to wait till it's ready. I wonder what Muse-like things I can do to help him along. Did Lou Andreas-Salomé nag Nietzsche about getting on with *Also Sprach Zarathustra*? Come on, Friedrich – or did she call him Fred? Freddie? Walrus-face? – you've been sitting at that desk of yours all morning...

Just be yourself, Stella.

We both want to make music together: he'll play piano; I'll sing. Alex suggests Schubert's *An die muzik*.

I need a little time to familiarize myself with it. This means waiting till nobody's about, then sitting at the keyboard and picking out the melody note by note – why couldn't Schubert write the bloody thing in C? Liszt watches me as I do this, and I make him promise not to tell Alex quite how poor my sight-reading is. In return, I give him a sachet of beef in jelly rather than the usual dried stuff. Then I discover that Alex has a recording (he might have told me!): I play it and hear something so different that I have to check it's the same piece.

Oh, well, as Stuart says, it's Not the Start that Matters, but How you Finish. We perform it one evening; I think I do rather well, but Alex says it 'needs work'.

We don't do much work on it, however, as he has a new project that seems to take up all his spare energy: a quartet to play twentieth-century chamber music. I ask if they need a 'roadie' and tell him about Lucy and the band, but he doesn't see the link.

They organize a performance – Alex doesn't like the word 'gig' – at St Ethelbert's. They practise hard, especially the Schönberg, usually round at ours. It's not really my kind of music, but I'm happy to do stuff in the kitchen, bring in occasional cups of tea, or console the cat, who is obviously scared of visitors.

The performance takes place. Hardly anyone turns up. I guess the venue isn't ideal: those seats aren't very comfy. But I can't help feeling the choice of music plays a part. I think back to when we filled this place with the melodies of Wolfgang Amadeus Mozart – and people. I remind myself how Alex made that all happen, how dreadful the orchestra was until he came along and breathed life into it.

Afterwards we go to the pub. Alex gets the first round, or rather pays for it out of the takings at the door, after which there is £5.43 left.

"This town's full of damned philistines," he mutters as he slams down the tray.

"Come on, Alex," says David, the viola player. "Contemporary music is a minority taste, but so what? As long as the folk who turned up enjoyed it, then we've done a good job."

"You get more people at a village football match than we did," Alex says. "What does it say about the sort of world we live in?"

"You should let me help with the publicity next time," I suggest.

Walter, the double bass player, mumbles a comment into his bushy beard. I'm not sure I've ever made out a word he's said, but Alex nods energetically. "Too damn right, Walter. All the 'publicity' in the world won't change how fucking pig-ignorant most people are. Jesus Christ…"

He says the word 'publicity' with a real sneer. The poor turnout has really hurt, I can see.

*

Next evening, it's Alex's 'proper' pub night. I like drinking with him, but I can't keep up: it's best once a week that he has a free hand.

I sit at home and watch TV, then suddenly, for the first time since coming here, I feel alone. I don't know why; it just suddenly hits me. I need to talk to someone.

I've not spoken to Lucy for a while. I know that's horribly ungrateful after the help she gave me, but this is *my* adventure, *my* life-changing experience, and Lucy does have a way of muscling in on things. But the moment I hear her voice – all jangly and Catford for the first few sentences then gently drifting back to her natural Sydenham – I realize how much I've missed her.

She tells me about a big gig coming up next week, in a field somewhere in Oxfordshire. And about her new man.

"He owns a record company!" she says.

"I thought you hated record companies," I find myself saying.

"Yes, well, that was when nobody would sign us. Anyway, weekend after next, we're off to LA."

"Los Angeles?"

"Yes, Stella. Los Angeles."

"I thought you despised Los Angeles. The dagger of capitalism thrust into the heart of a freedom-loving nation's creativity, you once called it."

"We'll only be there a month." She pauses. "Zavvy's not what you think, Stells. He's…" She pauses again. "Nice. Everything still wonderful for you?" she adds.

"Of course!" I reply. As I say that, I realize that's a lie, and that I'm phoning because the precise opposite is true. But I don't want to say that. I can't.

"Maybe we've both cracked it at the same time," Lucy says chirpily. "We could have some kind of joint ceremony!"

"Ceremony?"

"Yes. Why not? If we've both found The One… I've always rather fancied a handfasting on top of a mountain."

"Maybe." I'm not sure what handfasting is, but I sense Alex would not be into it. And there's a definite lack of mountains round here.

We talk a bit more, then she has to get ready, as Zavvy is taking her to some restaurant I've never heard of but apparently should have.

When I put the receiver down, I want to feel I have osmosed a little of my sister's happiness. But I haven't. I seek out my old phone book. Almost everyone in it is either a friend of Bobby's or someone I've lost touch with years ago.

Vee is now Mrs Jenkinson.

"Oh hello…" Pause. "How are you, Stella?"

"I'm OK."

"Good." Another pause. "You gave us all a shock."

"Oh. Do you think ill of me?"

"You're a friend."

"But if I wasn't?"

"That's a hypothetical question."

"People have to be true to themselves, you know."

"Even if it hurts other people?"

"Nietzsche said…" I begin, then run out of inspiration. "I suppose, sometimes, yes."

There's a brief silence. "How's the family?" I ask.

*

Alex gets back particularly late. I'm in bed, and I hear him clumping around the kitchen. I want him to come upstairs and be with me, but the clumping continues; I pull on my dressing gown and make my way down to where he's staring at the empty fireplace.

"Good evening?" I ask cheerily.

"No."

"Oh, er… What happened?"

"I did."

I don't understand what he means, but I put my arms round him anyway. He tries to push me away, then pulls me to him. We sit there for quite a while, then he lets out a loud belch.

"Overdone it," he says, getting unsteadily to his feet and wandering off to the kitchen. He reappears holding a glass of water. "I guess I'd better sleep down here tonight."

"No. You don't have to. I like it when you sleep beside me."

He turns to me and fixes me with a strangely ugly look. "I'm a such a bloody fool."

"What's happened?"

"Nietzsche was right. The Artist is a priest. A priest of the trans – trans – a priest of the sublime in a vulgar, sell-out world. God is dead; long live music. Proper music, serious music, that is."

"Absolutely!"

"No, Stella. You don't believe that at all. That's the problem. You believe in the way someone does who turns up at church on Christmas day, sings a couple of carols and comes away thinking how spiritual they are. That's not priesthood. Priesthood means sacrifice, dedication, sublib... blob..."

I never find out what else priesthood means, as he spills his water all over his trousers. "Oh, fuck it! *Fuck it!*"

I want to empathize with Alex. I want to know about the demands that his music makes of him. I want to know what lies at the heart of the Artist's anguish.

But instead – I can't help it – I get a fit of the giggles.

"Yes, hilarious, isn't it? Father Collings has been at the Communion wine again. And he has seen the light. Again. Again! Hallelujah!"

I start stuttering out an apology, but it's no good. "Let's talk in the morning," I say instead.

*

At 4.30 I'm in the kitchen making a cup of tea. Then I go into the big room, sit on the edge of a chair and stare round at the music, the books, at Alex, who slept on the sofa after all. His face has been released from last night's ugliness and looks beautiful again. Maybe you can only really know someone when they've made a complete chump of themselves in front of you. I head back up to bed and actually sleep a bit.

The alarm goes off at its usual time. I make breakfast – well, get some bowls out and put cereal in them. Alex sits down, stares into his Krispi-Flakes then at me. "This hasn't worked, has it?" he says.

"I'll do boiled eggs tomorrow if you like."

"I mean us, Stella. You and me. We live in different worlds."

"That's not true, Alex."

"It is true. You're one of those women for whom Art is a kind of plaything, a decoration, something that makes the world nicer and prettier."

"No I'm not!"

"I've lived this stuff. I've lain awake at night wrestling with the pain it causes."

"Tell me about it. Let me in. Let me see."

"I shouldn't have to. A truly cultured person would know." He sighs. "Your old teacher was right, Stella. *Be true to yourself.* I can't do that and live with you. It's as simple as that."

I try to summon a reply, but none comes. I try to look him in the eye (he looks away). I look round this place, that I have come to associate with love and truth and Art and –

"I want you to pack your stuff and leave," he says.

"Pack?"

"I can't stand long, drawn-out farewells. If something's over, it's over."

"Over?"

"Over. I'll call a taxi if you like."

"Taxi?"

"What do you want me to do, Stella?" he snaps.

"Give us a bit more time."

"Why?"

I run this scene over and over in my mind in the days after it, and come up with all sorts of clever, strong answers. But at that moment, I have none.

*

The landlady at the B and B helps me up the stairs with my universe.

"Good to see you back again," she says. "Give me a shout if there's anything you need."

A reason to live?

I fling myself onto the hard, lumpy bed and the tears well up. There is nothing to break their flow now – no shreds of dignity – so that's what they do now, flow, for what seems like hours.

Then, as suddenly as they started, they stop. I unpack the case – some toiletries, a few clothes, Malcolm's pottery shard (which I've kept in a box all these years, which probably says all sorts of dreadful things about me), a photo of myself with Lucy when we were girls – and arrange them on the bed. I love them so much! Then I can't stand their company a moment longer and must have fresh air.

I end up in a café near the bus station, sitting at a formica-topped table, sipping a cup of stewed tea and watching life go on all around me. Life. Real life: obese mums, tattooed dads, crop-haired boys with plastic toy guns, cutesy girls clutching anorexic dolls, grandparents old at 55 with poor teeth and stooping gaits. Lives far superior to mine, as they involve family, children, belonging.

Unexamined lives, the philosopher in me objects.

Lives, Stella. Lives.

A baby a few tables away starts screaming, and I have to be on the move again. A shaven-headed man with a ring in his nose holds the door open for me as I hurry out, and I'm so bloody lost in myself that I don't even thank him.

This time, I find myself at the train station. One of the books Dr Licht got us reading was *Anna Karenina*.

I shake my head angrily. But why not get *onto* a train and head back to London?

No.

What Alex said was unkind and stupid, but people say unkind and stupid things. Better than keeping it all bottled up, surely. When he comes round to apologise, we'll clear the air and …

Get real, Stella.

I get real. But I'm not going back to London. It would mean admitting failure to Bobby, to Lucy, to Mother, to Mr bloody Brown and his stuck-up daughter, to the Poly (or whatever it is now) as I creep past it every morning on the way to some shitty new job. It would mean watching the articulated death-wagons on the South Circular Road and hearing their invitations again.

I came here for a reason, I tell myself.

What reason?

That's what I need to find out.

I head for the river, where I sit watching a piece of rubbish bobbing along, and admiring its resilience. Then it sinks. I head back to the B and B via an off-license, where I ask for something cheap and alcoholic. The storekeeper recommends a peach brandy, which I take to my room and swig from.

It's rather nice, actually.

*

"Feeling better, Stella?" Stuart is dressed in a bird suit.

"Yes, thanks. It was just one of those 24-hour things."

"Good. Like the outfit?" The bird suit has stubby little wings and a long, conical orange beak that looks like a penis and that waggles uncontrollably as its wearer speaks. "Meet Osbert the Oystercatcher. The new mascot for Ingelow Town FC. Kleep! Kleep!"

I retreat into my office and switch on the computer. The accounts of Zzapp! Marketing suddenly fill my life with order and meaning – for about five minutes, then I find myself in tears again.

Several hankies later, the crying stops. When I'm sure my eyes aren't red any longer, I head for the coffee machine. Company, that's what I need.

Millie, one of the designers, is there. "Hi Stella. How's it going?"

"Fine!" I reply.

"Cool!" she says, taking her mug and heading off.

No. To receive consolation I must first admit loss. I hover by the machine, waiting for someone to appear. No-one does. The phone rings, which I'm supposed to answer. Someone else gets it. I stay hovering. I need consolation.

"Hello Stella." It's Richard, our IT expert.

"Hi."

"You don't look happy. What's up?"

Out with it! "My partner and I have split up."

"Bad luck." He takes a milk carton and sniffs it cautiously. "Some life-forms reproduce asexually. Sea-squirts, for example. I think that is a superior strategy. Do you think this milk is OK?"

I take the coffee back to my office and finish it. It is, as usual, revolting. But maybe it's all I'm worth.

"You OK?" Deanna, our chief designer, pokes her head round the door.

"Fine!" I reply, then burst into tears again. She puts an arm round me, and leads me across the hall to her office, where she puts me gently in a chair and goes and makes me a mug of proper tea.

An hour later, I leave her office, feeling consoled and clutching a book.

Twenty-Eight Rules for Getting over a Break-up

Rule One: Don't seek Solace in Drugs or Alcohol

OK.

But *Pêche Deluxe* helps to pass the time. I've got into a bit of a routine, now. Usually after work I wander round Ingelow a bit, then sit in the B and B 'guest room' watching soaps or quizzes on a communal TV until I remember I'm a Philosopher and Lover of Great Art. But when I get up to my room, I don't feel like serious reading, so a drink comes in handy.

It tastes nice, too. Maybe Dr Sharilee-Jayne Goodhart PhD (she's the author of the book) hasn't tried it.

Perhaps I'll send her a bottle.

Rule Two: Sort out The Practical Stuff: your Money, your Home.

Bobby's now being very sensible about it all, so this is easy. One day, he even calls to say that there's a small business issue we need to sort out. I own some shares in Mowatts, and he'd like to buy me out.

"Of course," I reply.

Dr Sharilee-Jayne Goodhart PhD hisses that I must be tough.

"A quid each?" he suggests.

Dr Sharilee-Jayne Goodhart PhD tells me to get a lawyer.

"If you think that's fair," I say.

Dr Sharilee-Jayne Goodhart PhD turns away in disgust.

"Send me the documents and I'll sign them," I go on.

So he does, and I do that, and a cheque arrives for five thousand pounds. That goes a long way in Ingelow. A deposit on a property, for example.

*

23 Fen Street has no hall – the front door opens straight onto the road. It is advertised as 'two bedroom', but the guest bedroom will only be of use if I have one of the Seven Dwarfs to stay (or one of the Six: I'm not inviting Grumpy). There are 'issues' with the plumbing, but I pretend the house is haunted by a friendly ghost, whom I start referring to as Wolfgang Amadeus.

Once I'm properly moved in, I hold a little party to celebrate. People from work, and… Well, just people from work, actually. They bring partners, which hurts a bit, but you can't not ask them. Stuart and Gemma bring a big bottle of Champagne, Deanna and Joe a book called *Ten Ways to Brighten up your New Home*. Even IT Richard turns up, with someone called Beth; the two of them spend most of the evening on my sofa snogging. It's a fun evening, anyway – as far as I can remember, as I drink too much.

But the bed I finally collapse into is *mine*. The toilet I'm sick into next day is *mine*.

<u>Rule Three: Get out there and Meet People</u>

Now I'm sitting in *my* front room, in a chair *I* bought from a charity shop, reading *my* book. 'You may not think so right now,' Dr Sharilee-Jayne Goodhart PhD tells me, 'but you have a lot to offer the world. Everybody has.'

I remind myself that she hasn't actually met me – but she's right: I ought to try. So I start looking around for things to do.

Line dancing.

Bridge.

Nothing grabs me.

There's a shop I pass on the way to work that sells long velvet dresses, bronze hookah pipes and pictures of Red Indians. One day, I see a poster in the window.

Ingelow Aquarians
invite you to
The Four Karmic Forces and Extra-Terrestrial Life
a talk by Dr Empyrion Pangelides
at the Clement Attlee Hall, South Street
7.30, Tuesday 11th
Entrance £1

I feel a sudden frisson of excitement.

Come on, Stella. Hardly serious philosophy, is it?

Pooh! Who says? A Frenchman with hair like a bassist in a heavy metal band? A sex-starved German with a walrus moustache?

This is *my* journey.

*

I'm nearly late – the Hall is rather hard to find – but there is still room. Quite a lot of room, actually. I take a seat and watch as a few more fellow seekers arrive. They all greet each other with affection. Maybe soon I will belong, too.

At about twenty to eight, an elderly man wanders out in front of us, picks up a microphone that starts hooting at him, stands helpless until someone switches it off, then turns to us. "Good evening, everybody. Welcome to our monthly talk. But first, a few notices…"

Several centuries later he announces that the business is concluded, and can we all please welcome tonight's speaker, Dr Empyrion Pangelides of the Cosmic Wisdom Association.

There. Wisdom: isn't that what philosophy is all about? *Philo – sophos.*

A muscular, bearded man strides up to the microphone. "Good evening, fellow seekers after truth," he booms. "I am from Outer Space!"

The audience nod politely. The speaker looks disappointed.

"I was joking, of course. But I might not have been. It's a well-known fact that beings from other worlds have been visiting our planet for many years. Maybe one of them is sitting among us now."

I nod. Which planet was I from? I've forgotten. Sure as hell wasn't Earth.

"First slide, please."

A blur appears on the screen behind him, which he slowly focuses into an old-master painting of the Annunciation. It is not as beautiful as some of the ones Dr Licht showed us, and it's upside down. When the slide is replaced the right way up, we see that the light pouring down on the Virgin is coming from a kind of disc, which could possibly be interpreted as a flying saucer.

"Note the *four* lines of light coming down from the craft," says Dr Pangelides. "Most observers see no significance in this – it's just a piece of artistry; four looks nicer than three or five. But, of course, it is *not* a coincidence. Ancient Masters tell us that there are Four

Karmic Forces at work in the universe. The first of these is called Zoanthropism."

Zoanthropism turns out to be something to do with the global ecosystem, I think (I find myself drifting off, wondering how Lucy and Zavvy are getting on). All living things have vibrationary frequencies, which can be in or out of harmony. 'Visitors' can sense these with ease. 'Terrestrials' can do so if we practice 'attunement'. There's a course Dr Pangelides runs; next one is in July and there are places still available. There's a special discount for us today.

After another Karmic Force whose name I can't remember, it's time for a break. The main lights go on, and a hatch in the right hand wall flies open. "Tea and biscuits," says a voice from behind it.

I start sidling along my row. The woman at the end shows no sign of moving, and I come to a halt and consider backtracking and going out along the next one, which is empty. Then she looks up at me and grins.

"I'm in your way, aren't I?"

"Well, er…"

"That means yes. Let's get some tea. My name's Sarah. With a P."

"Oh, Stella. Stella Tranter."

"Nice to meet you. Isn't he interesting?"

No. "Yes," I say.

"There are so many fascinating ideas around nowadays, don't you think?"

"I guess so."

"There are, believe me. We are entering a whole new era of love."

"Some of us are."

"Oh, we all are, Sheila. The Age of Aquarius is upon us – and not a moment too soon."

We join the queue.

"Last month we had a fascinating demonstration of Tibetan Singing Bowls," the woman goes on. I'm sure she said Sarah. "They're wonderful things. Quite wonderful."

"What do they do?"

"Sing."

"Bowls?"

"Well, they resonate. It sounds like singing. It's very spiritual."

They've run out of chocolate biscuits by the time we reach the tea-hatch. I take a Nice one instead. A man with a goatee beard comes up to us.

"Sheila, this is Doug," says Sarah with a P. "He's an expert on geometry."

"Geo – netry," he corrects her.

"Oh, yes, of course. A few months ago, Doug gave a most interesting talk about the pyramids in Egypt."

Doug fixes me with a stare. "The pyramids are magnets for geonetic forces. I'm hoping this chappie's going to talk about them in the second half. It's been a bit, er, superficial, so far, don't you think?"

"Well, I'm not – " I begin, but Doug is already ploughing on.

"The people who built the pyramids possessed technology that was way superior to our own. How do you think huge, forty-ton blocks of stone were raised hundreds of feet above the ground?"

"Perhaps they got lots of people to – "

"They used geonetics. The inhabitants of Ancient

Egypt, or *Misr* as it should properly be called, used giant gongs, or *hmbs*, made of bronze – the exact formula for their manufacture remains a mystery. They were struck with giant beaters, or *qlfs*, and the sound waves were directed to drive the stones up ramps of wood. To do this, the waves need to be channeled geonetically. There's no other way."

I have to get away but don't know how. So I just stand and listen, till the old boy who made the announcements starts pinging the side of a teacup with a spoon and asking us to return to our seats.

"That's really fascinating, Doug," says Sarah with a P.

"Yes it is," Doug replies.

*

In the second part of the lecture, we learn the nature of the Third and Fourth Karmic Forces, how these relate to the Twelve Signs of the Zodiac and the Eight Chakras (not seven, as the ill-informed think), then, of course, the Uniting Principle behind them all. Love.

"Any questions?" Dr Pangelides asks at the end.

Doug's hand shoots up. "I don't quite see how this fits in with the theory – and practice – of geonetics."

"I'm not sure what you mean, sir."

"Surely you know Elliot Tandberg's work on geonetry?"

"Geometry?"

"No, Geo-netry. The Science of Geonetics."

"Oh. No. Er…"

"You should read it." Doug then commences a description of Elliot Tandberg's work. A very thorough description. After a while, the man who pinged the teacup interrupts. Has anyone else any questions?

Nobody answers.

I guess I feel sorry for the speaker, who, despite having reached the Tenth Level of Attunement, is looking dazed. I see Doug limbering up for another question and stick my hand up.

"Why is love so important?" I blurt out. "It seems to me the most unreliable thing in the world. Is everybody in this room madly in love?"

An embarrassed silence falls.

"The Masters are more thinking of love on a cosmic scale," says Dr Pangelides.

"What the fuck does that mean?" I snap back.

People turn and stare.

Doug asks another question, and Dr Pangelides suddenly says he has no more time. The teacup man announces that next month will feature a talk on the Lost World of Atlantis and can we leave the room tidy.

As we go out, everyone avoids me.

*

"Shame on you," mutters Nietzsche as I walk home. "How could you fall for that rubbish?"

Descartes nods in agreement.

I round on them. 'What would you do instead, then? Stuck here in the middle of bloody nowhere because of my stupid pride and my complete bloody inability to conduct relationships? Come on, clever-clogs. What would you do? Bridge? Line dancing?

They fall silent.

"I would try line dancing," says Descartes.

Nietzsche nods. "Yee-hah!" he adds.

Rule Four. Give Yourself Treats

Dr Sharilee-Jayne Goodhart PhD says that giving oneself Treats repositions one's Locus of Control from Without to Within.

One day I see a young woman cycling down Southgate Road: she has a joyous smile and her hair flies out behind her like a streamer.

There's a bike shop in the town centre. My Treat is sky-blue; she has six gears, a real leather saddle and panniers at the back to put picnics in. She's called a Queen Roadster.

I don't just ride Her Majesty around town, but start exploring the flat land that surrounds Ingelow. People say the Fens are ugly and unlovable, but I soon realize they have their own special beauty. They have vast cloudscapes, black earth, untamed wind, and geometrical lines of poplars, power-lines and reed-filled dykes, which lead the eye and the mind to a horizon as flat as the sea. With this flatness comes a sense of boundlessness, of possibility.

My love for the Fens grows with each outing. That, I tell myself, is how love should be.

Rule Five. Remember that you will Slip Back sometimes.

Dr Goodhart talks about 'dips'.

I get a lot of those. Some mornings, I wake up cheerful and stay that way: Alex was just a walk-on part in my life, whose role was to bring me here so I could start being really true to myself. But just as often, he barges into my thoughts the moment I wake up and I have to drag my sense of loss around all day, like a stone inside my soul.

You just have to ride the dips out, Dr Goodhart says.

They are tests of the new you that you are creating. I get that. New me. Fen-cycling, Zzapp-marketing, 23-Fen-Street (complete with ghost) owning...

One day, I'm in High Street, heading for the Oxfam shop where I've noticed a rather nice throw to put over my sofa. And who do I see coming out of the town's only record store? It really is him, too I've had a number of false sightings, but this is the real thing.

Decision time. Should I:
    a) Ignore him
    b) Saunter up and say 'Hi' in a cheery, I'm-over-*you*,-mate-y sort of way?

Ignoring seems rather passive. I start sauntering.

A woman follows him out and hands him a bag. He flashes a smile at her and takes her hand. "Poor cow," I chuckle knowingly to myself.

Then I feel a pain as if someone has kicked me in the stomach. My saunter turns into the briskest walk I can manage – in the opposite direction. This turns into a run the moment I am out of his view, and stays a run all the way to 23 Fen Street, where I scrabble with the keys, slam the door behind me when I finally get in, sink into my sofa and start sobbing. The sobs are deeper even than those when I first lay on my bed in the B and B. They rack me as if I'm trying to vomit up something vile and alien.

Come on Stella, calm down. It's a dip.

It's a precipice. Up to now, I realize at once, I have held my truly deepest feelings back. I've been pretty miserable, but nothing has felt like this.

So now, I guess, I really am being true to myself.

And this means...?

The thought comes to me in a moment: it means absolutely nothing.

Maybe the reason that Alex didn't love me was because there wasn't anything to love. 'To thine own self be true' – but supposing there isn't anything to be true to? Supposing 'I' – the old I, the new I, all the Is that have ever paraded round with a label marked 'Stella Tranter' on them – am just an endless succession of selfish, meaningless, momentary needs and emotions? Me, want, now. Me can't have, fall apart. No centre, no purpose, no 'Cartesian' point.

"I don't think I could live if I really thought that," I say.

"No, you probably couldn't," Earl replies.

I get slowly to my feet, and they lead me into the hall and place me in front of the mirror, which I rarely look into (I just thought it looked nice there). I look into it now and see... nothing.

Well, something, obviously. But it's a mask. I actually pull at my cheeks, to see if it will come off, but it doesn't. It can't, I realize, because behind there is nothing for it to come off from.

Or maybe it's worse. Not just 'nothing' but an actively negative force, a vampirical, clawing emptiness, with an endless need to suck truth and life and vitality from others. Poor Bobby had years destroyed by this monstrosity. Alex, wiser, escaped it: no wonder he threw up the shutters so quickly, so totally. But it just carries on needing and needing, pretending to love 'Art' or 'Philosophy' or 'Beauty' but actually just seeking some kind of confirmation in these things. But, of course, it can't find any such thing, because there is nothing to confirm. It is – I am – nihilism made flesh.

I burst out of the door. I unchain the bike. I pedal furiously onto South Road, crashing through gears and red lights past puzzled Ingelowers. Sorry I can't stop; a pack of demons is after me. If they catch me, they will rip me to shreds – if there is anything to rip.

*

I do stop, of course. I stop when I'm exhausted, when I can't pedal another metre, when I'm miles out in the Fens, somewhere and I don't care where, as there's nowhere I'm going anyway.

"All right, take me, you bastards," I mutter to the demons as I slump forward over the handlebars, heaving breath in and out of my lungs. "You win. Finish me off. I deserve it. I'm evil… useless… pointless…"

Nothing happens.

The wind puffs in my face.

A seagull screeches.

I straighten up and look around. What's that on the horizon?

It's the spire of Cawston church. I expect to feel another boot in my guts, but instead there is a surge of joy.

Once, I felt love. Real, blooming, grand-hearted love, not this doomed, bitter, wizened, soul-sucking nothingness.

So? That was then…

But it was real at the time. I *was* once something, so I can be again, surely.

I loved, therefore I am.

I begin to ride towards the village.

<u>Rule Six, Rule Seven (and so on).</u>

Pooh, I don't need these. I have a point of certainty.

Stalking

I cycle out to Cawston most evenings, now. Into the village, across the top of Common Road, then on to North Beach or looping up through the fens to Notby or Sea Pining. I nearly always get a 'moment' like the one where I spotted the spire, when I know I am real after all, not a soulless vampire.

Part of me is aware of how ridiculous this pedalling round in search of Cartesian moments of self-confirmation must seem – to someone else. But *I am a unique being, only once on this earth* and to me, it is the essence of staying sane.

When the days shorten, I force myself to cut my trips down to weekends only. I find I can live with this. Just. During the week I work hard: business is brisk in the world where people make things, sell things, buy things, are Always Positive and dress as Osbert the Oystercatcher. Evenings it's TV or cooking, the recipes as complex and engrossing as possible.

However, one Sunday I follow my usual bike-route and get no 'moment'. I tell myself I cannot force them – that's the point; they just come, and that's what makes them meaningful. But what if the supply runs dry for good? Will nothingness creep up on me and drag me back to the despair and self-hatred that I felt in my front room? If it does, I'll have no way out this time.

By Wednesday I can't stand any more, so take the afternoon off, pleading a migraine, and do the ride. This time I pause at the top of Common Road, take a deep breath and slowly pedal towards Alex's. Opposite number

58, I recall how we once set out on a walk but only got this far when a huge black cloud blew up... I feel that moment of full-on loving and being loved back, and am OK.

A couple of rides later, of course, this location no longer delivers a moment. The memory has become expected; to work it has to surprise me, to jump out at me. But that's fine, as I pedal on to number 44 and the garden ornaments – gnomes, windmills, toadstools and wide-eyed cats – that Alex used to be so wittily rude about. Then it's number 38, with its tatty wooden notice board advertising a British Legion Jumble Sale from eight months ago. Then finally, I'm forced to grit my teeth and pedal right past number 26.

I loved, therefore I am.

*

One day, his car isn't outside the house.

Curious, I coast to a halt and stare at the front door. Behind it will be the big room: the fireplace, the books, the Art, the sofa.

I shake my head, but find myself wheeling the Queen Roadster up to the next lamp-post, propping Her up there and walking slowly back.

Crunch, crunch. I'm at the window and can see inside. The rugs. The Persian one he really liked. The red one by the fireplace – for some reason that was my favourite. It's a bit faded, and Alex wanted to throw it out; I said he ought to move it somewhere more central, next to the piano – but didn't insist, of course.

I spot my reflection and jump.

This is getting weird, Stella.

But it is necessary. The alternative is being that soulless

nothing in the mirror.

*

A few weeks later, the car isn't there again. I take Her Majesty over to the lamp-post, lock Her there, walk back... At the side of the house is a weatherboarded gate. There are no sounds from the back garden, so why not take a look? If a car draws up, the sound of the gravel will alert me. There's a hoppable fence at the far end, straight into fields.

The moment I'm through the gate I know this is a marvellous thing to do. Maybe I can gorge myself on memories and not need to come back for a long, long while. That bench we had to be so careful sitting on – it really is falling apart, now. That bed with about 150 species of weed. The gnome – pure post-modern irony, of course; Alex's *hommage* to number 44 – under which he used to keep a back-door key.

I wonder... Yes, he still does.

Well, I'm here, aren't I? Why waste an opportunity that may not recur for ages? I know exactly how to fit the slightly rusty but still workable key into the lock, and exactly how far to turn it.

Like this. Click.

I am inside the house.

A quarter-read novel by someone I've never heard of straddles the arm of his favourite chair. There's cat hair all over the place. The fiddle isn't even in its case, just sitting on top of the piano.

I go over to the sofa and sink into it.

I wander into the kitchen, where the same old mugs hang from the same unevenly spaced hooks. *Berliner*

Musikfest 1987. He's a bit low on milk, I notice. Maybe he's just popped out to get some more. No, the village shop is closed on Sundays and he'd hardly go all the way to Ingelow for a pint of milk. When we went out at weekends, it was for long walks. We'd often not get back till it was dark. Sometimes we'd go straight upstairs afterwards...

I climb the stairs and push gently on the bedroom door, sit down on his side of the bed, stroke the pillows, bury my face in them. The smell is instantly familiar.

I'm not sure how long I spend up here, then suddenly it is enough. As I turn away, I wonder if this will be a turning point. Maybe I'll never have to come back.

I make my way downstairs again. A last look around. My glance falls on the violin. I want to hold it just one more time. I pick it up, with intense care, and feel its lightness.

The moment I do, I know that all shall be well. I can reconnect with all my noblest aspirations. I shall live fully, authentically, by the finest standards, by the standards I found in Philosophy and Great Art. They will support me: me, Stella, a self I can be true to, not in a vain, showy way but one which is strong and true and beautiful and proud and –

Crunch.

Wheels on gravel.

I jump with fright, and the violin... Well, it just seems to leap out of my hands. I make a despairing grab for it, but that only sets it spinning, so when it hits the flagstones it does so with extra force. A crack echoes round the room. Its arched brown back has a long split all the way down the middle.

Stay calm, Stella.

'I just happened to be passing by, and remembered I'd left something behind, and – '

I panic. I run.

Walking

I don't stop pedalling till the point where the road rises up and runs over the old sea-wall. There, exhaustion finally gets to me. I stop and dismount – well, virtually fall off – flop onto the grass, then glance back at a very distant Cawston.

Nobody's following.

I heave a sigh of relief, then realize how ridiculous that relief is. I must go back and explain. A shiver runs through me at the thought of quite how embarrassing this is going to be, but it has to be done. I pick myself up and turn the bike round. I put my foot on the pedal and poise myself to move forward.

Nothing happens.

Just put your foot down on that pedal, Stella.

I can't.

So you're just going to run away, are you?

No, I'll…

…*cycle* away. I turn the bike round and coast down the far side of the old sea-wall towards the sea.

I tell myself this is cowardly and dreadfully wrong.

I ride on.

At North Beach there's one vehicle in the car park, one of those round-looking ones that old men drive. No sign of its owner. Perfect. As I prop Her Majesty up against a litter-bin, I run a fantasy in my head, that a nuclear war has broken out and destroyed all human life the other side of the old sea-wall. Now there's only me and one old man, and I'll find ways of avoiding him. There will be no more emotional entanglements, nothing more to get wrong, no more embarrassment, no more inadequacy, no more other people to have standards that I fall perpetually short of. A world without people = a world without pain. Simple. Logical.

I need to walk. The tide is out, but I want to see the sea close-to and be as far from the people-cursed land as possible.

I set off, and soon get to the first mark of the October spring tide – just a few days ago, it must have been – plastic bottles, rope, bladderwrack, bleached pieces of wood (one of them looks uncannily like that violin lying broken on the floor). Then I reach a section where shells crunch underfoot. Then they are replaced by beautiful, half-flooded ridges of sand. Then there's a bit where my footings turn to mush. Then it's firm hard sand again.

I'm now at the start of a spit that juts all the way out into the sea, which is still a long way away, but audible now, a gentle but insistent whoosh. To my left, the sand merges into a kind of lagoon, calm and sparkling. To my right, a miniature cliff drops into a choppy, deep-looking current: the mouth (I guess) of one of the little rivers that wind through the dunes. In front of me, the spit divides, one branch peeling off to the left to enclose the lagoon while a peninsula of sand runs straight out seawards, where it vanishes beneath a criss-cross of breakers.

I set myself targets – a boulder, which I soon reach; a buoy; a bright-green ribbon of kelp. Only at the last of these do I ask myself exactly why I'm doing this, but I get no reply other than that I want to, so walk on.

I am now near the end of the peninsula. Small waves

lick either side of me; ahead they merge with deceptive neatness, and beyond that are the real breakers. There's spray in the air now, and the sea makes a range of sounds: *boom* as a wave topples over, *hiss* as it hurls foamy water across the gently sloping sand, *suck* as it retreats to meet the next breaker rearing up behind it. The wind joins the racket by buffeting my ears; it has become deliciously strong out here.

With each pace, the sea is nearer now. Soon I am yards from the line of spume where the waves exhaust themselves. I stand and watch the wind pick at it, then a big roller comes in and pushes the spume to the tips of my toes.

I'm filled with a strange, ecstatic pleasure, which I do not understand.

And then I do.

I want it all to end here.

The whole bloody charade, the endless loops of running and hiding, the biggest one of which has just connected perfectly to the negation of its own beginning: the one that began in that cramped little room in the Polytechnic and has ended with me smashing a perfect symbol of all that room offered.

But it hasn't looped round totally. One tiny strand, one theme, is still free and mine. I still have choice. I can choose crawl, shame-filled, back to land where I will be ripped to shreds, not by demons but by the world for my egotism and stupidity – or to merge myself gloriously with this booming, boundless power that is rolling itself out in front of me.

I begin to walk out into the foam, to where the next

one is drawing itself up for its moment of self-immolation. I shall be immolated with it, and that will be a moment of becoming. A true Cartesian point.

Boom! As the water cascades towards me, I will it to sweep me away, to merge me with its might. I choose to die gloriously, willed and willing, free at last from –

Don't be such a bloody idiot, Stella!

I spin round and begin splashing furiously back towards the land. The falling wave grabs my calves with its ice-cold claws, at first pushing me in my new chosen direction, then, pretence over, dragging me seawards. For an instant, its pull is so strong that I don't think I can resist, but I dig in and the pressure is gone. When its successor follows, I have outpaced it. Soon I'm on dry, solid beach.

I give a sigh of relief and sink to my haunches, staring out at the sea that is now just a rather noisy object. Quite impressive if you like that sort of thing. I begin to laugh: great heaving laughs that I don't think I've ever laughed before. First, I have no idea what I am laughing at, then I know that it's at myself – and that if I can laugh at myself then all this nonsense about non-existence is ridiculous.

Get back home. Get back, sort out the mess you've got yourself into and get on with your life. Your beautiful, beyond-price life.

I laugh some more, then rub my eyes. Then I'm ready to return to confessing to Alex, to sorting out any damage – whatever the cost, I'll pay – to finalizing my divorce, which wasn't caused by my egotism but by the simple, sad coming together of two human beings who thought they were made for each other but who turned out not to be. I'll even get 23 Fen Street's plumbing fixed, though I'll miss

Wolfgang Amadeus.

I turn and start walking, proud as a cat, towards that crazy but beautiful circus we call life.

Ah.

While I was busy having my existential revelation, the tide has sneaked in between me and the land.

There must be twenty yards of it: once land, now water, with little clue as to the lie of the sand beneath it. I know that to the left, the ground tumbles into what will now be a deep, fast-flowing channel. I recall that to my right the footings were soft and treacherous. So I just have to head straight, I suppose. But will it be that simple?

When the tide comes in, it's so fast.

Just do it, Stella. Right now, or it will be too late.

I start wading, and soon head too far right and find myself in gloop. So left a bit, but not too far – fall into that channel and I am gone: dragged down, choking, struggling – will I see my life flash before me?

It doesn't bear thinking about, so don't.

More steps. All good so far. But then I feel the pressure around my feet getting stronger.

Ignore it. Keep walking.

I am, I guess, about half-way across when a wave smacks into my calves and nearly knocks me over. I turn and see breakers rolling across open water where that nice enclosed lagoon once was.

So? I just have to keep going. I brace myself for the next wave, take its pressure, then have a few moments to shuffle forward before the next one hits. I curse it, and my fury gives me energy.

Keep going, Stella. Step, brace, take the next wave.

Step – it's deeper– am I going too far left? I try and look through the rushing water but it's unclear now. So I must fix my eyes on a landmark – that old car is perfect – head for it, and hope. Brace. Take the pressure...

The water swirls round me. Its waves roar like a train. Its spray stings my eyes. It's making my clothes damper and colder with every moment. Brace, take the pressure, step – Please God, let there be enough time (please *who*, Stella? Shut up and get on with it) – thankfully no deeper. Brace, take the pressure, step –

Into nothing. I tumble forward; my hands scrabble for sand and find it. Water cascades over me. I feel it lift my body and heave me forward, but mercifully not into the channel. I hack out a lungful of brine and force myself back to my feet, just in time to withstand the next wave. But I'm shaking now. I'm sodden. I start shivering. I start to wonder which wave will get me. This one? The one after that? The one after that? Dry land seems further away than ever – it *is* further away than ever, because the tide is flooding in – and the water between it and me is deepening with each second.

I have no choice. The thought comes that maybe freedom is not about having choice but about *not* having choice. It is knowing that you have to fight for something with every atom of your body. I won't go down without a fight – now, or ever again.

Brace, take the pressure, step. My body is screaming that it can't go much further. I scream back at it that it bloody well can and bloody well will, and that seems to stop its complaining – for another step at least. And another. But I can't scream myself safe for ever. Brace, take the pressure…

The next minute or two feel like a lifetime.

Brace, take the pressure, step.

Maybe they are a lifetime.

Brace, take the pressure, step.

Then suddenly my next step is clearly shallower.

Don't get your hopes up. Keep fighting.

The next one is shallower still.

You've not there yet, Stella. Keep at it.

Another big wave comes in. Brace, take the pressure. I roar insults at it, and it is past me. I step forward again, confident suddenly.

And then it is over. The waves are spending their intensity behind me and I'm striding through the water, splashing in shallows, yelping and whooping with the joy of a child.

Someone has appeared on the beach. I fall silent, suddenly embarrassed. The person runs towards me. He stops by the water's edge and holds out a hand; I stagger up to him and grasp it.

"Are you all right?" he says.

"Fine, thanks." Of course I'm fine.

Who does he think I am? Some idiot who lets herself get caught by the tide?

I collapse at his feet.

Falling

I'm sitting in the old car, wrapped in a travelling-blanket; the engine is running and the heater on full blast; I've got water all over *Seabirds of Britain*, drunk all this guy's coffee and eaten both the jam doughnuts he'd bought for his tea.

"I still think I'd better take you to the hospital," he says.

"No. I just need to get home, that's all."

"You're sure?"

"Yes. I'm already amazingly grateful for what you've done."

"We all have to do our bit, don't we?"

"I... guess we do."

We set off.

"What happened to you?" he asks, just as the car is coming up to the old sea wall.

"I didn't notice the tide coming in behind me. I'm new round here."

We reach the top of the wall, run along it for a few yards, then begin our descent.

"Actually, that's rubbish," I go on. "I tried to kill myself. Then I suddenly realized what a bloody stupid idea that was."

He nods. "Very wise. I got very depressed when my wife died a few years ago. I'm not sure it got as bad as walking out into the sea – but I felt pretty low. I went and saw a therapist. She got me to face up to things. Well, to face up to myself really... She gave me some business cards. I don't think I've got one on me, but I can drop one round to you if it would help."

"That would be kind," I say, though I have this deep sense I won't need therapy. Not now I've faced the October North Sea. But I give him my address anyway.

"It's always worth battling on, you know," he adds.

"Yes, I do know."

*

The moment I get home, I make a cup of tea, then flop joyfully onto my bed. I am asleep almost at once. I do not dream, but wake in the middle of the night.

I look round at the window and the ghostly outlines of my little bedroom.

I am experiencing these things.

I am alive.

I'm breathing, I'm sentient, I'm dry, I'm warm, I'm here, I'm Stella, I am therefore I am.

*

Alex.

It has to be done. I'll offer to pay for repairs, of course. Whatever is right (a concept that suddenly seems to have no philosophical ambiguity to it at all).

Her Majesty is still out at the beach, so I take the bus to Cawston. I think of the woman who used to cycle along this route, desperate for a moment of sanity amid the madness that swirled around her, and feel pity for, and complete distance from, her.

But of course I still feel nervous.

We stop outside the Crusoe Arms. Nobody else gets off. As I walk down Common Road, I try to do so with confidence and calm. He'll understand, I tell myself. It was an accident. Maybe he'll appreciate my honesty in coming forward. I want him to know what I've been through in the last few months. Not to make him guilty, but simply to tell the truth. My truth, shared and worth hearing.

Then the nerves stab back in. To give myself one last piece of determination, I imagine wading through that water. *I won't go down without a fight – now, or ever again.* I crunch across the gravel and knock on the door.

It opens. Alex is looking at me with a puzzled expression. "Hello..."

"Hello, Alex. I've come to apologise."

He says nothing for a moment, then his jaw drops.

"It was you... Jesus Christ!"

"I'm so terribly sorry, Alex."

"Sorry...?"

"Yes, I... It's awful, I... didn't mean..." I'm getting incoherent.

"You bitch," he says, slowly and clearly. "You fucking bitch. I... can't think of anything more horrible than that, Stella. Anything more egocentric, more petty, more vindictive, more spiteful, more – " He begins to lose it, then calms himself.

"It was an accident, Alex," I say, calming myself, too.

"An accident? What do you mean?"

"It wasn't deliberate. You don't think I...? You can't..."

"What were you doing in my house?"

"Yes, I know it sounds odd. I just happened to be passing by, and remembered I'd left something behind, and as you weren't exactly friendly when we parted company, I thought if I let myself in and took it, that way there's be less embarrassment and…"

I stop.

"No," I say. "The truth. I was going crazy. There was this hideous emptiness inside, and the only way I could stop it eating me up was to – "

"Oh, for God's sake," he says, and slams the door. His voice calls out from behind it: "Wait there, please."

I rehearse the story. He has to know. Maybe start at the record shop, or how I felt when I saw the spire, or…

He's back at the doorway, holding out a piece of paper at arm's length. "Read this and sign, please."

I take it; the moment it is in my hand, he pulls his away with a gesture of revulsion.

I, Stella Tranter, am responsible for the damage for the Donati violin and will pay for any repairs necessary or for a replacement if the instrument is irreparable…

"Well, of course I'll do that, Alex. That's part of what I've come round to say. I don't need to sign a piece of – "

"Sign it."

"I haven't got a pen."

"Don't get clever with me. Wait there. If you're not there when I get back, I'm calling the police."

"Alex…" I protest, but the door has already shut.

I stare at it till it opens again. "Here." Alex is shoving a pen in my direction.

"Thank you," I say, out of habit, then sign the paper. "Look. It all started when – "

"I'm not interested, Stella."

"I want you to understand!"

"I want you to fuck off out of my life and never have anything to do with me again. Anything. Ever. Now give me that bit of paper back."

I hold on to it for a moment, realizing that it gives me power. Then I hold it out and he snatches it. Power to do what?

"This was you to a tee, wasn't it, Stella?" he says. "The real you. Deep down inside, you loathe culture for being beyond you. You're worse than those dickheads in Ingelow who ignore it altogether – at least they stick to their melodramatic soap operas and pathetically predictable Abba records, and don't pretend that they belong anywhere else." He grimaces. "But you… You, Stella, are the ultimate phoney, the ultimate enemy of all that is good and truthful. Your narcissistic, empty little ego lies its way into somewhere it thinks is shiny and beautiful, then systematically sets about dragging everything around it to its own infinitely vacuous and selfish level. You should have stayed with your stupid punk rock band or your dull, golf-playing little husband, instead of trying to fool everyone with your ridiculous Philosophy and Great Art act."

He smiles, but in a way that radiates fury. "I guess I'm grateful to you in some way, for showing me how deep some people can sink. It's quite a consolation really. But don't think this means I'm going to just walk away. You will get that fiddle fixed. You will put back every little bit of decency and truth you have tried to suck out of the world."

The smile broadens. "You'll probably hate doing so. I hope you do, Stella. God, I hope so. I hope you wake up every morning feeling acutely aware of how small you are and how big the world of True Art and True Beauty is and how you will never get close to it in a hundred years. And I hope it hurts like hell. Every damned moment." He pauses.

"My solicitor will be in touch. Now fuck off."

The door slams.

"You're wrong," I say to it. But my voice is weak and unconvinced.

So I simply stand and stare at the door, then turn and trudge back to the bus stop. There's another one in three hours.

*

I must say sorry properly. Show him that those things he said aren't true. I sit at my desk and fill my waste-paper basket with versions.

I manage something decent, finally. Something human, real and not self-pitying, but not bland or pushy either. Something really 'me'. I walk to the end of Fen Street and balance the letter on the lip of the postbox, recalling how I felt when I first wrote to

26 Common Road
Cawston
Ingelow
AT29 8QX

"Bring calm and peace," I ask it.

*

The reply comes a week later.

P. Sproule represents Alex Collings of 26 Common Road, Cawston, Ingelow, AT29 8QX. She has a document, signed by me, admitting damage to her client's property and accepting all liability. Repairs have not proven possible. Sourcing and purchasing a replacement instrument of commensurate quality will cost £20,000. Will I please contact the office to arrange payment. In the case of non-compliance, a criminal complaint will be made to the police and formal proceedings to obtain the monies will be commenced forthwith and pursued with full force of the law (and so on for several pages).

On Saturday I go down to London and visit some music shops. £20,000 for a Donati is 'a bit on the high side', I learn, but it's hard to price quality instruments. One chap who seems interested in my story tells me that I need to check that the violin is totally irreparable: restorers can do great work these days. He also recommends I get legal help.

First thing Monday morning, I get out the Yellow Pages.

"Can you hold a moment please?" says the receptionist from the first solicitors I call.

Music begins. Vivaldi's *Four Seasons*.

I put the receiver down.

Come on, Stella! *I won't go down without a fight – now, or ever again.* Remember?

But fighting would prove him right. It was my fault, after all, even if it wasn't the deliberate act of vandalism he has decided it was. It was my doing, so I'll pay the price.

Hell, it's only money.

*

"It's only money!" I say jokily.

My bank manager gives me a look as if I'd just announced I was from Pluto and did he mind if I parked my UFO in his ashtray. "It's a great deal of money, Miss Tranter."

"Yes, but… I have to have it."

He glances at the sheet I've filled in, showing my income and outgoings. "You say you have some equity in the property."

"Yes."

"Sell that first, then come back to us."

"And where will I live?"

"There are cheap options, Miss Tranter. If you really need that money, you will take them."

I tell him I'll think about it, then wander idly through town hoping a magical escape route will present itself. But of course there are no such routes, just estate agents.

TO LET: Mobile Home.

It doesn't look too awful. In the end 23 Fen Street couldn't be my protector. No agglomeration of bricks and mortar could have been.

*

I sit on my old sofa my first evening in 57 Sunny View Park, noticing how damp the place is and listening to the couple next door having a row.

I don't care. I got myself into this mess; I'll get myself out of it.

Rule One. Avoid any future emotional entanglements. Nietzsche, I recall, lived alone in a boarding house for ages. OK, there was all that Lou Andreas-Salomé stuff, but he must have got over that. I will be like him, steadfast, alone and untouchable.

A sound like a saucepan being thrown across a mobile home comes from next door.

Rule Two. Do something about soundproofing.

*

Stuart bounds into the office one day saying that we are sponsoring a group of musicians called the Fenland Orchestra and isn't this a wonderful opportunity to raise the profile of the business. I can't remember my exact comment, but he replies that I'm being negative. Zzapp! Marketing is a Negativity-Free Zone, he reminds me. I apologise.

Two days later, Stuart announces that the orchestra has decided to go with another sponsor, Fizz Publicity. Apparently one of their committee went crazy when he heard about the deal, and insisted on changing.

"I don't know what we did wrong," Stuart says, with a shrug.

Just before Christmas, he calls me into the office again. One of our biggest clients is moving their account to Fizz. The MD is a great fan of classical music and has been particularly impressed by what Fizz are doing with the orchestra. As a result, Zzapp! are having to cut back. He's so sorry. I've been a great team member. They'll pay me till the end of the month.

They give me the rest of the day off, too. I ride out to North Beach. Well, I creak, as my new bike isn't a patch on the Queen Roadster, who had disappeared when I went back to fetch Her. I come here quite a lot. It has become a place of solace, a place of self-renewal, a place where, when things get tough, I can remind myself of how much worse they could have been.

I sit on the sand, stare out at the sea – and feel no solace or self-renewal at all.

"Hello again."

I turn round. It's my bird-watcher.

"Did you go and see Emily?" he asks.

"No, er, I lost the card. I, er…"

"It took me a while to pluck up the courage, too."

"It's not…" I begin.

"I'll drop another one round. On Fen Street, weren't you?"

"I've moved. 57 Sunny View Park. They're really quite nice, those mobile homes," I add.

He doesn't look convinced.

Roaring

The bike makes a snickering sound as I wheel it up the path, as if it's delighted at quite how hard it has made my journey here. By the doorbell is a little brass plaque telling me I've come to the right place.

I park next to a large black wheelie bin and secretly hope that the dustmen will come in the next hour. Then I return to the doorbell, where I pause for a moment. Do I really want this?

I close my eyes and press. There is a deep ring from inside the house. Footsteps.

"Stella?"

Emily Reid, Therapist, is older and softer than I expected.

"Do come in," she says gently. "Can I take your coat?"

I wonder if she will be able to take my madness. Perplexed teenagers, yes. Old women who have lost their husbands, yes. But stalkers who go round smashing vintage musical instruments…

"Come this way," she says, and shows me into an airy room where she invites me to choose a seat from a circle of three. We run through a few procedural matters – payment, confidentiality – then she smiles, adjusts her posture and looks me in the eye.

"So, Stella, tell me about yourself."

"Well…" I begin, then dry up. The room is not airy at all, but crammed full of embarrassment.

"In your own time."

The embarrassment is forcing itself down my throat. I

feel myself reddening. I start to sweat again.

"It's nothing," I say suddenly. "I'm fine. I don't know why I came here, really. Nice room you've got here. Those curtains…"

"Tell me about yourself, Stella," says Emily, with a new firmness in her voice.

"I…" I fall silent, then burst into tears.

Once I've dried my eyes and begun talking, it all floods out: Bobby, Alex, seeing him coming out of that shop, the stalking, that bloody violin… And nihilism and Dr Licht and Philosophy and Great Art and –

"Our time's nearly up, Stella."

"What? An hour?"

"Fifty-five minutes. I have another client coming at six."

"Bloody hell. I've just talked, haven't I?"

"Yes. Talking is good."

"It is, isn't it?" I smile, then look at her earnestly. "So what's wrong with me?"

"You are depressed, I think."

"So I need to cheer up?"

"You need to change, Stella."

"What to?"

"I've no idea. My job is to help you find out."

*

"I want you to roar, Stella."

It's our second session, about half way through. Emily tells me to stand up, stretch out my hands into space and make the loudest noise I can.

I do my best.

She looks dismissive. "That's not roaring, Stella. That's

saying the word 'roar'. I mean really roar. With joy. From your very depths."

"Supposing I don't feel any joy or have any depths?"

"Pretend you do."

"All right." The sooner it's finished, the sooner I can get back to telling him about getting ditched by Malcolm.

I roar.

"How did that feel?" Emily asks.

Actually it was rather nice, but I don't want to let her win that easily. "Yeah. OK."

"Then you won't mind doing it again. Even louder this time."

All-bloody-right. "Roar! Roar! Roar bloody roar, bloody RRROOOAAARRR! Happy with that?"

"You seemed to be, which is what matters. I recommend doing that every day."

"The neighbours would hear."

"Let them. Now, this Malcolm fellow..."

I don't care any longer. It was a long time ago.

At the end of each session, she gives me homework to do. Along with my daily roar, I have to give myself a weekly treat, like going to the cinema or for a walk in surroundings I find beautiful. I have to keep a diary of 'affirmative' thoughts that leap into my mind, and write them on post-it notes then stick them around my home or at work. She suggests some:

I am a decent person.
Nice people can make mistakes.
Change is part of life.

"These are so Californian!" I protest.

"I know," she replies. "People have all this fun in

California, don't they? Sitting on beaches, playing guitars, enjoying the sunshine. Ugh! We're so much better here in Britain. We can be really miserable. That shows how deep we are, doesn't it? So Artistic, so Philosophical."

"Fuck off." (Emily says I shouldn't hold back in expressing myself.)

But during the week that follows, the caravan fills up with notes.

I quite like them, actually. No, Nietzsche probably didn't have *I'm OK and other people are OK too*' (in German, of course) stuck on his fridge. But would he have been happier if he had done? Maybe he would even have made it with Lou?

I get in my daily roars, too. Not as loud as Emily would like, but she lives in a solid brick house, not one whose walls seem to be made of plastic.

*

We don't just talk and roar; sometimes we do what Emily calls 'interventions'. One time I have to hit some pillows to 'get in contact with my anger'.

I give them a gentle tap.

"I don't want to damage them," I explain, when she says I should hit them harder.

"Yes you do."

"Don't tell me what I want," I snap back, and whack the things, out of frustration, not because this woman has told me to do so. But it does feel rather good, so I do it again. And again. And again...

"I needed some new ones anyway," she says at the end.

"Sorry about the language," I reply.

Other times he has me sitting on a third chair

pretending to be a string of 'significant others' in my life: Lucy, Mother, dad (a gap), Malcolm, Bobby, Alex (who still takes more time than anyone), Mozart, Descartes, Nietzsche, God. (Emily says it's best to cast the net wide.)

Sometimes I swap chairs, and these avatars get into discussion with one another. In one session God and Nietzsche had a real ding-dong, one calling the other a Nazi and the other covering his ears and shouting 'You don't exist anyway so I'm not listening to you'.

Outside the therapy room, I find happiness seeping into my life. It comes in unexpected places, uninvited. I suddenly find myself realizing I've not been miserable for at least half an hour. And when things go wrong, I feel less and less that whatever triviality it was is not the thin edge of a wedge that will ultimately propel me back to that awful darkness, but just, well, an annoyance. OK, there is backsliding from time to time, especially about half-way between sessions. Saturday evenings can be bad. I feel madness prowling round the caravan, trying to get in. The brandy helps then. I've promised Emily to give up solitary drinking, but she also tells me that I don't have to be perfect.

So, overall, I sense that my life is changing.

To what?

Emily claims he has no idea – it's my journey, she says – but I don't believe her. What does she know that I don't?

*

One session, I ask her what the philosophy is behind what she is doing.

"These sessions are about you, not me," she replies.

"That's therapy-speak."

"I'm a therapist."

"I need an answer."

"Why?"

"I just do."

"I'm interested in why you need to know this, Stella."

"Oh, for God's sake, Emily, I just want to know, OK? Will you tell me?"

"All right. Do the roaring exercise again."

I do, at full volume plus a bit so she can't complain that I'm not trying properly.

"That's my philosophy," she says when I'm done.

*

At the end of that session, I have to go into her study to write her a cheque for the next six ones.

The room only has one bookshelf, on which sit a number of rather dry-looking texts on therapy, a set of thrillers, some cookery books and a Manual of Home Improvement. No great literature or philosophy.

In the corner is a CD holder, a tall wire rectangle with a wire cat's head on the top and wire cat's paws sticking out of the side – a gift, I assume, from a grateful but taste-deficient client. I check out the contents.

Emily has them in alphabetical order. So the Abba CDs are at the top. Above Phil Collins, Christopher Cross, Neil Diamond…

I glance up at the mantelpiece, where a familiar sight greets me: a red-roofed cottage, a wagon crossing a stream.

I tell myself that when my bike needs repairing, I don't ask if the repairer reads classic literature, listens to Mozart or has original taste in art.

*

"You don't listen to classical music, do you, Emily?"

It's about five minutes into the next session.

"No."

"Why not?"

"These sessions are about you, not me, Stella."

"Emily…"

"OK. I find it rather dull."

"Dull?"

"Yes, dull. You've taken a peek at my CD collection, I assume, so you know what I enjoy. 'Soft adult contemporary' is the official industry classification, I believe. I find the music restful and reassuring after dealing with people's pain all day. Did you like the holder? I got it in a second-hand shop."

"It's… different."

She nods. "I'm afraid classical music doesn't do it for me. I find it repetitive and rather… tinkly."

"Tinkly?"

"Yes, tinkly. I can't think of a better word. Of course, Alex wouldn't approve of those sentiments, would he?"

"No."

"Or Dr Stanislas Licht."

"No."

"Or Wolfgang Amadeus Mozart."

"Well, obviously not."

"And Stella?"

I pause. "No," I say finally but firmly.

"Good. It's one of the things I like most about my work: no two human beings are the same. So why should we all like the same books, or paintings, or music?"

"Great Art is superior, Emily."

"That's an opinion."

"It's a truth," I reply.

"Who says?"

An answer forms, then seems to die on my lips.

"Some philosopher?" she suggests.

"No," I snap, then add, "Well, yes. But what's wrong with that answer?"

"My experience is that whenever someone starts talking about philosophy, they're trying to hide something. It's called over-intellectualization."

"So Descartes and Nietzsche were just 'trying to hide something'?" I say witheringly.

"I don't know. I've never had them sitting in this room. But I'm not very impressed by what you've told me. This business about having one point of certainty in one's life? Why, for heaven's sake?"

"Because, logically, there is no alternative."

"Maybe logic is wrong, then," Emily says with a shrug. "Supposing there are hundreds of points of certainty? Or none at all, just life, going on all round you, which you're best off just living?"

"So don't ask questions; just be dim-witted and accept everything everybody says?"

"Ask loads of questions, be highly intelligent, don't accept anything if you don't want to – but don't expect a pat, logical answer to emerge at the end. Just live."

"How?"

She shrugs again. "Do things you like doing. Be nice to people. Smile: did you know that people who smile a lot live an average of 5.3 years longer than those who don't?"

"Gosh, how deep," I say, even more witheringly than

my last piece of witheringliness.

"OK, that was a little homely. But it's better than 'Be utterly selfish. To thine own ego be true'."

"That's not what Nietzsche meant!"

"Maybe it isn't. I've not read him. But it seems to be what he can end up meaning. He's got the same problem as Monsieur Descartes. *One* answer. But supposing the total opposite is correct? Supposing there isn't one self to be true to? Supposing, instead, that we have lots of selves, all of them 'us' in some way or other'? Some are wonderfully noble; some are deeply damaged; some are dull but useful in day-to-day life. Maybe we just have to work out how to navigate our way around them, to be one Stella at one moment, another Stella the next."

"How do you know which one to be?" I say – rather cleverly, I think. I'm not going to lose this one.

"Maybe you just learn." Emily smiles. "I sense you're afraid that if there wasn't this great logical structure in place, everything would fall apart. But maybe it wouldn't. Maybe there's enough vitality and goodness in the world – and in you, Stella – to hold it all together."

"Supposing there isn't?"

"Supposing you just have to trust?"

"Trust what?"

"Just trust."

"That's nihilism!"

"No, Stella. Nihilism is *not* trusting."

I pause to take this in. "You think philosophy is a waste of time, don't you?"

Emily shakes her head. "It can be a very interesting hobby. Hobbies are important. My brother Felix derives enormous pleasure from his collection of stamps. He's got hundreds of them, all neatly arranged in countries and categories and 'mint' and used and – "

"Philosophy opened wonderful doors for me," I snap.

"You're using the past tense, Stella."

Looking

I have to make this journey.

I take a couple of days off work. On the first afternoon, I visit Mother: she tells me how she saw Bobby on Dulwich Common the other day. He's doing very well – his firm was taken over by Americans, and he got pots of money. Didn't I have some shares? I could have been rich. He's seeing Bill Carr's younger sister, now, by the way. Such a nice, sensible girl. Down to earth.

"That's great news," I interrupt. "Do congratulate him... No, maybe best not. But I'm really happy – for both of them."

Mother shakes her head. "I don't understand you, Stella. I really don't."

That makes two of us. But I don't need more negativity: tomorrow, I must be clear-headed and bright-spirited. I head off to the cheap B and B I've found near the old Crystal Palace, then next morning walk to my destination.

*

KNOWLEDGE FOR ALL.

The old inscription is still above the gate, though a greenish mould is settling over it and it is now partially obscured by a neon sign welcoming me to the U IVERSIT O CATF RD.

I feel a lump in my throat. Of excitement? Of loss? Or maybe I'm just irritated by the fact that they can't be bothered to fix the bloody sign.

There doesn't seem to be anyone at Reception, so I

pause to remind myself of the way to the Music Department, then go there. The corridor is a tasteful beige and has been newly carpeted. From the Departmental Secretary's office comes a soft whirring. I knock at the door. No reply. I pause, recalling the last time I stood here, then knock again louder. Still no answer. I push the door and it opens to reveal a girl who looks about 12 encased in a set of earphones. She looks up at me, removes the phones, smiles and asks if she can help.

"I'm trying to find Dr Stanislas Licht," I say proudly.

"Licht?"

"Yes. This is the Music Department, isn't it?"

"Music?" She looks at me as if I have asked for Splidgology or Advanced Pogglorifics. "This is Business Studies. I don't think we have a Music Department..." "Music..." she says again, still baffled. Then her eyes light up. "One of our lecturers wrote something about brand identity and product life cycles in the record industry. Is that what you're after?"

"No... I'm sorry... Thanks anyway."

I walk slowly back down the corridor – past the doctor's old office. The door is half-open and there's nobody inside. I can't resist.

It looks about twice the size I remember it, but I guess that's because all those books have gone – as have the piano, the violin, the music stands, the scores, the loose sheets of music paper, the reels of tape, WA Mozart, the tape-recorder with Bakelite buttons. Now it is sparse, tidy and smells of air freshener. OK, there are some books: they are on finance and have been corralled onto two shelves which they share with a coffee machine and a photo of a rather drunk-looking group of men.

I sit down on a plastic chair and close my eyes. I can hear the Doctor's voice now:

In their heart, everyone knows well enough that they are a unique being, only once on this earth, and by no extraordinary chance will such a marvellously picturesque piece of diversity in unity as this ever be put together a second time. That's you, Anna, and you, Stella…

I feel the thrill again. I move the chair to where I used to sit. Next to me would be Anna. Where is she now?

Not divorced, unloved, temping, up to her ears in debt, living in a caravan and seeing a therapist for depression, I suspect.

Another voice:

Deep down inside, you loathe culture for being beyond you. You're worse than those idiots in Ingelow who ignore it altogether – at least they stick to their melodramatic soap operas and pathetically predictable Abba records, and don't pretend that they belong anywhere else…

I start scrabbling in my bag for a handkerchief.

"Are you OK?" A young man in a Lacoste T-shirt and white trousers has entered the room.

"Yes – I'm sorry – I – It's…"

"Let me get you a drink of water."

Suddenly I want to tell him all about Dr Licht and the group.

He listens with only occasional glances at his watch. "Gosh, I wish I had that effect on my students," he says finally. "We still have a philosophy department here. Would you like to visit them?"

"No."

"You should. I'll take you over there. My name's

Julian, by the way."

"Oh... Stella."

We head down the corridor.

"Look, I really don't want to go to the philosophy department," I say as we reach the first set of swing doors. "They... didn't approve of the stuff I just told you about. They caused trouble, and got the course cancelled, actually."

"Even more interesting. What was this chap's name again?"

"Licht."

"We must try and find him."

"We?"

"I'm absolutely fascinated."

We try the phone book and directory enquiries – no joy – and end up in the office of the University HR Department, looking through old employment records.

"Here we are. Licht, Dr Stanislas. 38 Somersham Road."

Of course!

"And there's a phone number – even though it's an old 01 one..."

We call its updated version, but it is unobtainable.

"I'll go round there," I say.

"I can take you there, if you like."

"No. I..." Julian has become entranced by the Licht magic, but I must go alone, just me and my confusion and my pain. He looks disappointed when I tell him this. I try to explain, probably fail, and offer to buy him lunch afterwards instead, promising to report back what I have found.

*

It's a bus ride (still the 197) then a short walk to Somersham Road – just as it was all those years ago when Anna, Noddy and I went to see him. The street is drab, though a few houses have clearly been smartened up. One has a big yellow skip outside it full of rubble, old carpet and bits of furniture.

Number 38 is one of the drab ones. I knock on the dusty, peeling door, which might have once been blue but is now just a kind of grime colour.

No answer. I try and peep through the windows, but they are filthy. I knock a few more times. Silence.

I try the neighbours either side. Nobody in. Then a house across the road. Finally, another knock on grubby old 38. No reply.

This is pointless.

*

Julian insists we lunch in the Senior Common Room. "There might be some old-timers who remember your Doctor." We join a queue. "Any faces you remember?"

I look around. "No."

"What about names? Who taught you?"

"Well, there was Dr Peabody."

"Never heard of him."

I feel a vengeful delight: I may have turned out a loser, but *your* reputation hasn't lasted either, has it, Peabrain?

I know; I'm being negative. I try and think of some more names. "Dr Spigott?" I say, though he's probably teaching in North Korea these days.

"Of course!" says Julian. "I should have thought of him. David Spigott-Jones has been here for ages. Head of the Economics Department. One of the most radical free-market thinkers in the country."

"Different guy," I laugh.

"No, same guy. He underwent a conversion in the eighties. *The Marxian Myth Exposed. The Great Leap Backwards: the Crimes of Chairman Mao.* You could ask him about Dr Licht if you like. He's over there."

"You mean the chap with the quiff and the bow tie?"

"That's him."

"I can't believe it!"

"It's true."

Looking at him now, it is true. Cut the hair, shave the beard and the droopy moustache, send him to an expensive tailor... The moment we get our food and find a table, I'm across to where the former Dr D Spigott is tapping at one of these new PowerBook laptops.

"Oh, er, excuse me... Professor Spigott-Jones... You don't know me, but I'm hoping you can help me."

He glances up and eyes me with a look of distaste.

"I'm... trying to trace an old lecturer here," I continue. "Dr Stanislas Licht. You were a young member of staff when he retired. Do you remember him?"

"No." The professor returns to his PowerBook.

I turn round. Julian is flapping his hands at me in a gesture that I assume means something like 'don't be such a total and utter coward!'

"I'm such an admirer of your work, Professor. *The Marxian Myth Exposed* really spoke to me."

"Which part in particular?"

"Oh, all of me... I was *so* hoping you might remember something about Dr Licht."

"What did he teach?"

"Music."

"We got rid of that lot ages ago."

"This *was* ages ago. There was a particular incident where he got into trouble for running an extra-curricular philosophy course."

"I don't remember, I'm afraid." He goes back to his computer.

"That's such a disappointment. I so enjoyed *The Great Leap Backwards.*"

He lets out a sigh and stares into space. "I do recall something. Lots of extra-curricular stuff. Irrationalism. The powers that be stopped him, of course... And some silly little girl kicked up a huge fuss about it. We had to throw her out. Just as well; she was a raving Trotskyite who'd have had the rest of us hanging from lamp posts."

"Do you know what happened to him?"

"Sorry. I really have no idea. He's probably sitting in a home for retired liberal arts lecturers in Eastbourne doing the *Guardian* crossword. Subsidized by you and me, in our capacity as taxpayers, of course. I'm assuming you pay tax; you don't look like a sponger."

"Can you think of any way I might find him?"

"I really can't. Sorry." And then he goes back to the computer.

"Well, it was worth a try," says Julian. "Do you want some pudding? The treacle tart is actually quite reasonable."

He gives me a spare key to his room – he's lecturing this afternoon, then has a meeting with a software consultancy interested in sponsoring part of a new MBA – and tells me to 'make myself at home'. I sit there with a mug of coffee from Julian's machine (he reckons the stuff from the SCR is even worse than what you get in the student refectory).

I remember listening to the Requiem as a young man, and suddenly knowing that I had found something that I could build my life around. Something solid, something absolute, a glowing source of inner power that would never let me down.

Then I'm sitting on my sofa in 23 Fen Street, feeling that hideous nothingness. I see the smashed violin on Alex's floor. I hear the roar of the waves on North Beach. I hear the hatred in Alex's voice.

Where were you, Doctor, when I really needed you?

And you, Nietzsche, and you, Descartes, and you, Wolfgang Amadeus Mozart? You were quick enough to criticize me when you thought I was falling short of your standards. Come to me now, and tell me it's all OK, that you have messages for me about truth and beauty, right and wrong, love and hate.

There is no response, of course. Only…

I am a decent person.
Nice people can make mistakes.
Change is part of life.

*

When Julian gets back, he asks me how I'm feeling.

"Better," I reply.

"Good." He pauses. "Would you care to join me for dinner this evening?"

"That's awfully kind… But I feel I'm imposing on you."

"Well you are, but I seem to be enjoying the experience." He smiles. A winning smile – one, it suddenly occurs to me, that I could easily fall for. Could I really feel love again? The thought is electrifying.

"This isn't some pick-up routine, by the way," he goes on. "I'm very happily living with a man twice my age. That's him in the photo, in the middle of the group – the one with the particularly stupid expression."

"He looks nice."

"He is, really. But don't tell him I said that."

Julian gives me his address, and I say I'll be there at 7.00.

As I walk out past the old inscription, I have no lump in my throat, just relief in my heart. Here's my KNOWLEDGE: it's time to say goodbye to Philosophy and Great Art. Let Descartes have his unique, logical point of certainty. Let Nietzsche have his authentic, self-validating inner life-force. Let Wolfgang Amadeus Mozart have his hotline to the transcendent. Me? I am an accountant / office manager. No, I don't have permanent employment at the moment, but that will change; I'm good at these things. I live alone in a 'mobile home' in an end-of-the-line fenland town, but I live; I am not a bloated corpse floating face-down in the North Sea. I'm seeing a therapist for depression, but the therapy is working. I caused accidental damage to a valuable old violin, but I'm paying it off, every penny, because it is the right thing to do, not because I had lawyers chasing after me.

This is who I really am. These are the selves I must be true to.

Suddenly even the exhaust-filled air of Waldram Park Road has a touch of spring to it. There's devil-may-care in my stride as I walk up to the bus stop. Bang on cue, a big red double-decker appears.

It's a 197. No use; to get back to the guest house I need a 28B.

I jump on. I must have one last try.

*

Passing the house with the skip, I tell myself that the owner has had the courage, intelligence and energy to throw the old contents away. Throw away, Stella, not cling on to. Look at that desk. It's quite nice, but it's been chucked, because the inhabitants of 62 Somersham Road have got a better one. That's what change means.

I walk on to number 38 and knock.

Silence.

Of course there is.

Well, I had to give it a go. I turn, and head back down the street to my new life, which is my old life minus illusions.

There's a rattling noise behind me. The door of number 38 opens a crack. A beaky face peers out, as wizened as an old apple and with a deeply suspicious expression, but still unmistakably…

"Dr Licht?"

"Who are you?"

"I'm one of your former pupils. Stella."

He shows no sign of recognition. Well, of course not. It was two decades ago.

"I just wanted to come round and say…" I'm suddenly aware I have no idea what I want to say. Then I do. "Thank you. Thank you for opening doors for me. I'm afraid I didn't use the doors at all well, but that was my fault – well, 'fault' isn't the right word; I didn't do anything outrageously bad, just made a bit of a bish of things. But they were my mistakes, so I'm proud of them, because they've been part of making me who I am, and – "

"*Sind sie Deutsch?*" he interrupts.

"Deutsch? No. *Nein. Ich bin* Stella. *Eine von...* One of your pupils."

"Pupils?"

"The... Enlightenment Club."

"Ah! Quick!"

A bony hand grabs mine and pulls me in. I step over piles of junk mail and local free newspapers. A stench hits me, of rotten food and urine.

The Doctor flicks a light switch – I notice his other hand is clumsily bandaged – but no light goes on. "You're very brave," he says. "Coming here. Von Schirach has spies everywhere."

He clears some books off a chair and gestures for me to sit down. I suddenly feel desperate for something to say, then notice in the corner –

"That old tape recorder! You played us music on it."

Licht shakes his head. "It's broken. Long ago."

"Oh. So you've got everything on CD, now?"

"CD?"

"Do you have any means of listening to music at all?"

"I know all the tunes." He begins to la the opening bars of the *Requiem*, then asks, "Can I make you some tea?"

"That would be lovely. But why don't I do it?"

"No! The kitchen is untidy." He shuffles across to the same door he strode over to twenty years ago. As he opens it, I glance crockery piled up beside a sink; an overflowing waste-bin and a bowl of fruit covered in grey fur.

*

It's time to go.

"So, see you tomorrow at 10," I say. I'll be back with some proper cleaning materials.

"Yes, yes. It's very kind of you."

"Not at all. We Enlightenment Club members must stick together."

"True. True."

At the door, he holds out his uninjured hand. I take it and squeeze it; he tries to squeeze back and half-succeeds.

*

Julian and I do all we can to find if Stanislas has any family in the UK. No joy. I speak to Social Services, and a stream of different individuals comes to look after him for the odd half hour a day – when he will let them in. I start visiting at weekends, doing a bit of cleaning, dusting the shelves and shelves of books (reading them in the breaks, of course), shopping, cooking, showing him *again* how to use the CD player I bought him, checking that he's eating properly and is taking his pills. During the week, Julian pops round the odd evening. As a result Stanislas seems much better: a lot of the time he's quite 'with it'. But that won't last, of course.

I talk to him about trying a home: panic fills his eyes, and he starts talking about people who vanished in 1938 and never reappeared.

I stay with Julian over these weekends. He has a big house that his mother left him. He and Bill let me clear out an attic and stick a bed in there, after which Bill calls me Mrs Rochester. At first, I do a bit of stuff around the place to feel better about all this hospitality – but in the end, I insist on paying him something, after which Julian says I might as well move in.

I hand back the keys to 57 Sunny View Park with pure pleasure, though I do feel a twinge of loss as we drive back through the Fens (Julian has hired a van and is helping me move). But my future is no longer in Ingelow. There are plenty of lively small businesses in South London looking for good, permanent accountant / office managers.

Once a month, I go back to see Emily. On one visit, she says I should do some writing and 'get my story out'. I'd find it deeply therapeutic, apparently. After that, I spend a couple of evenings in Mrs R's attic staring at an old notepad and don't even know where to begin.

There's no point. It's old stuff. Over. Done. History.

Music Every Nite

It's summer. Proper summer, too, with real sun and real heat. I'm walking home – how nice to use that word and to know how much I mean it – from 38 Somersham; I suddenly feel thirsty; I'm passing a pub and suddenly think 'Why not?'

Because I was brought up in the belief that nice women don't go into pubs on their own, that's why not.

Inside, the place is dull rather than rough. The only thing I actively dislike is the landlord's spelling: *Music Every Nite*, it says on a board behind the bar. I run my eyes idly down the list of performers.

On Tuesday 24th, the featured act is The Jeff McFadden Band.

*

I ask Julian to come with me but he says he can't stand ageing rock bands. Bill can't stand rock bands of any age.

I'll go on my own, then.

"It'll be appallingly loud," says Bill.

"I'll bring a roll of supersoft loo paper to stick in my ears."

"It's a grotty pub."

"Fine, I won't buy a Versace outfit."

"It'll be heaving with forty-something former punks with beer bellies, pretending that it's still nineteen seventy – whenever punk was."

"1976. Look, I'm going, OK?"

I turn up at 8.00, the scheduled start. There's gear on the stage but no musicians yet. I order a glass of wine. A man with not too much of a beer belly walks up to the bar and takes the seat next to me. Suddenly I'm desperate to tell him about 1976.

He catches my eye. "Julie?"

"No."

"Oh, I'm so sorry. I'm supposed to be meeting someone called Julie."

I nod. The conversation should end here. But I want to talk. "So, you're a punk at heart, then..." I begin.

"No. I hate punk. All that swearing." He makes a kind of sucking noise through his teeth. "I didn't realize it was going to be that sort of stuff. They normally have quite decent music here."

A woman approaches us. This is probably Julie: I never find out, as the lights go down and a man strides onto the stage, Fender Telecaster in hand. I recognize him at once, though he's ditched the 1976 gear (except for a small silver ring in his left ear) for a check shirt and denims. It suits him. Three others follow: a bassist, a drummer and a keyboard player.

Jeff walks up to his mike. "Good evening everybody. Thanks for coming along. We'd like to start with a number called *Falling*. It's about love, and how it can go wrong and," he gives a shrug, "all that sort of stuff."

The keyboards begin with some swirling chords, then the guitar cuts in, decisive and rhythmical but no machine gun. Jeff starts to sing. I'd forgotten what a good voice he has: deep and full of emotion. The bassist puts in harmonies for the second verse, then the keyboard-player makes it three-part for the chorus. It's thought-out and measured in a way that the Fuckwits never were, but it still has some of the old band's... I don't know. What's the word?

Anyway, I'm mesmerized. Once a few people have ventured onto the space in front of the stage to shake their bodies about (rather half-heartedly, I feel), I even join them and dance. Why not?

The more I dance, the more beautiful the music becomes. It surrounds me; it lifts me; it tells me that life is full of beauty and purpose, and that I've always known that really.

After the show, Jeff sits at the front of the stage, selling CDs and chatting. I wait till the queue begins to shrink, then tag onto the end.

"Nice moves," he says when it's my turn.

"Thank you." I pause. "Don't you remember me, Jeff?"

He thinks for a moment, then his eyes widen with pleasure. "Lucy!"

"It's Stella, actually."

"Oh, Stella, forgive me. It's been a long time. What are you up to?"

"Working. Divorced. In debt," I say, then realize what a miserable old bag I sound. "But I'm fine, really. How about you?"

"About the same, actually."

"Gosh, I thought you and Annie..."

He forces his mouth into a smile. "It didn't work out."

"Oh, sorry."

"These things happen." He grins. "I've got my music. I'm fine."

"It's... really good."

"Not quite the old stuff, eh?"

"No. But it's still got... oomph."

He smiles. "Oomph! I haven't heard anyone use that word since – well, you last used it. You're one of a kind, Stella."

I find myself blushing and ask what happened to the other guys in the band.

"Tel went back to driving lorries. He still plays a bit – country and western I think he does now. Earl did a degree in Media Studies. Then he gave up drugs. Now he's a local councillor. Keeps telling me I should vote Liberal Democrat."

"You're still in touch with him? After what he said?"

"I heard a lot worse in Belfast. How is Lucy?"

"She's engaged to a rich American. They live in LA. Los Angeles."

"I do know where LA is, Stella."

"Sorry, I…"

Jeff is grinning, and I find myself grinning too.

"Lucy and I chat on the phone," I go on. "But… It's a different world."

He nods. "And what about Stella?"

"Oh, I don't know. I'm just me, really."

"Best thing to be. Come on; give us a hand with this speaker and I'll get you a drink."

*

Jeff takes me home in his van – I ask him in, but he says he doesn't leave gear parked in the street. I say I'll see him next week – they're playing at a pub in Hackney. He says that if I turn up, he'll play *Moon River* for me. I say I won't miss it for the world.

"You look cheerful!" That's Julian, who's up late marking essays and sees me coming in.

"Yes. I've had a nice evening."

He puts on a face.

"Just a nice evening," I tell him.

But when I get up to my room, I stand on my bed and roar. Not too loud, of course: I don't want to wake the neighbours.

September

I take my place in the circle of chairs, and spread my things out in front of me. My A4 Notepad, all clean and fresh and ready to be written on. My posh pen, a present from Jeff, who thinks this is a brilliant idea (not that I need his approval to do anything, but it's nice to get the support). My beret – I saw it on Lewisham market the other day and thought, why not?

A young girl is next to me, so I turn and say hello to her. "I'm Stella," I add.

"Oh... I'm Zeenat."

"Exciting, isn't it?"

"Yes!" my youthful fellow-student says with sudden enthusiasm. Then her face fills with nervousness. I smile at her, and she seems reassured.

"Nice beret," she says, after a pause.

"*Mer* – Thank you."

Further conversation is prevented by the sound of the door opening and the entry of the course leader.

I've been wondering what a writer would look like, but decided not to have any preconceptions. Flavia Cauldwell is smart, with expensive-looking shoes and an even more expensive-looking scarf draped insouciantly over one shoulder.

"Good evening everyone," she says in an aristocratic voice. She goes through the organizational stuff – fire exits, loos, etc. – then grins. "Writing is, above all, something you do. So let's get started."

My notepad's blankness is suddenly terrifying. I stare

round the room, then out of the window. We are actually across the street from the main building, so what I see is the South Circular Road, with its usual two-way traffic jam. Has it inspired much literary brilliance? Right now, I'd settle for one half-decent sentence.

I blame Julian. He told me about Catford Uni's 'outreach' courses. After an initial unwillingness to go within a hundred miles of them, I found myself leafing through the brochure one evening and suddenly wanting to sign up for the whole lot. *Introduction to Philosophy?* Maybe not quite yet. Next year? This time I've gone for *Life Writing*. Emily keeps going on and bloody on about me 'getting my story out', so it seemed the obvious choice – until about three minutes ago.

Everyone else has started. Zeenat seems to have covered the best part of a page with her big, loopy handwriting. My paper is still as blank as the day it left the A4 Notepad factory. Then Flavia spots me, which makes it even worse.

"Difficult, isn't it?" she says.

"Y – yes," I stammer.

"Good," she says and nods. That's all. Good. But she says it with a smile, and suddenly I feel laughter rising up inside me. I try to suppress it, but it won't be suppressed – out it comes with a snort.

I expect they'll throw me out. Oh, well, it won't be the first time.

"Oh, that's even better!" Flavia adds. She gives me a tap on the shoulder, then turns to the next pupil.

Now I'm more confused than ever. But I can't just get up and leave. So I escape by looking out of the window again. Actually, it's not only the South Circ I can see, but the front gates of the main building. Behind the neon sign, which they

still haven't fixed, is that old inscription.
>KNOWLEDGE FOR ALL.
>My pen begins to move.

THE END

Thank you for reading this book. I hope you enjoyed it.

If you did, I'd be very grateful if you would rate it on amazon (or wherever you bought it) or leave a review. Nice reviews help authors sell books and stop them going bonkers.

Please head over to my website, too. It's chris@chriswest.info.

My other fiction is a bit different to this. I've done four crime novels and some rather sillier (but, I think, fun) fantasy things. I write non-fiction, too: history and psychology. And, since lockdown began, poetry.

Happy reading!

Printed in Great Britain
by Amazon